Jessi

It's *you* - first + foremost.

And Then It Was You

Be exquisitely kind to *you* + Love

HEATHER STRANG

will flow in abundance.

♡ xx Heather ♡

as if I had never walked
except with you, my heart,
as if I could not walk
except with you,
as if I could not sing
except when you sing.
-From Pablo Neruda's *Epithalamium 3*

For Alison, Amanda, Ashley & Bethany
My first true loves.

ACKNOWLEDGMENTS

At this time in consciousness, more of us than ever have the opportunity to create intimate partnerships that are truly Spirit-Led, that truly honor the other and are based on not only a deep love for one another but a deep desire to live the fullness of this human experience – together – growing deeper into Love. Never before in history have we had this level of awareness, connection to Spirit and ability to break out of the old paradigms of Love and relating that have kept so many of us small and out of alignment with what it means to truly Love another.

We also have the opportunity to use all of the above to connect in ever deeper ways in our sexual intimacy – above and beyond transactional exchanges – to truly experience the spiritual connection that is available to us as Spirit's in a body through sexual intimacy.

Do not let this time go unnoticed or unexplored. Call in the Love of your Life. Allow yourself to abandon settling for "good enough" and make a focused intention to experience the Highest Level of Loving and sexual intimacy that is available to you in this lifetime.

I want to thank all of those who inspired this story through my own experiences with intimate relationship and through my connection to my Spirit Team, including the JOGs (see more at http://heatherstrang.com/blog/love-blog/) who guided me to share this beautiful story.

Huge shout-out of immense love and gratitude to my 4 younger sisters – Alison, Amanda, Ashley and Bethany – who's dynamic is featured in Allie's relationship with her 4 sisters. I love you girls more than words could ever express and I am grateful every day for our Soul and blood bond. Thank you for inspiring me to be the best big sister and woman that I can be. It has long been my desire to make you girls proud and for you to know how much you mean to me. And thank you to Alison & Bethany for bringing Hayley, Cayden & Trey into the world.

I feel so blessed to be their auntie.

Big love to my beta readers – Stephanie, Aimee, Kristin & Rachel – your feedback and Love of these characters and this story was so inspiring. Thank you, thank you. And so much gratitude to Christy Collins Medley on her perfect book cover design – you nailed it!

Much Love & Blessings to all who Love me, believe in me and support me on this wild, delicious, orgasmic ride of life. I am so excited to see where Spirit leads us to next!

XoHeather

1

He had asked for the divorce so abruptly that it caught her off guard. They were sitting at their small, maplewood kitchen table just like they had done for the past five years – him with cereal, black coffee and the newspaper, her with green tea, two soft-boiled eggs and a journal. He looked up from his paper and said in a tone one might use to make a comment about the weather.

"I don't want to be married anymore Allie."

It took all of her strength not to spit her green tea out right there and then. She looked up at him, her deep hazel eyes quickly filling with tears. She wiped her hands on her jeans, brushed a few sandy blonde flyaway strands from her face, cleared her throat and said, "Okay. So what does that mean exactly?"

Of course she knew exactly what it meant; she merely hoped to buy some time to regroup and make sense of what seemed to make no sense at all. Sure, he had been distant for months now and was spending late nights at work. But that happens. And sure these late nights did seem to coincide with his off-hand mention of a newly hired twenty-something sales rep, Stephanie.

But even so, it hardly seemed like the right thing for either of them to completely throw in the towel on their marriage. Especially over a twenty-something. Or any something for that matter. Their love was real and their time together mattered. Besides, there was therapy, relationship focused energy work, couples' retreats and a whole host of other things she had never tried but was sure could help them.

He stared back at her, his once luminescent blue eyes now surprisingly cold and icy.

"This isn't working for me and it's been something I've known for a while. I just didn't know how to tell you. I'm sorry Allie, I can't be married anymore."

His chiseled jaw and dark brown curls – features she used to love about him – now appeared sharp, angry and foreign to her. She gasped for breath, shocked by how easy this all seemed to be for him. He appeared perfectly calm and in control. The only way she knew that he was feeling a little something more than his icy stare and tone indicated was the tap-tap-tap of his spoon on his cereal bowl in between each bite. (And yes, he had somehow still managed to continue eating breakfast in the midst of this conversation.) The only other time he tapped his spoon this way was when he was on deadline for a story at the *Coast Reporter* that covered the entire Oregon coastline or if his editor gave him more than the usual amount of trouble.

"Marcus, do you hear yourself?" Allie would often say to interrupt his rap-tap-tapping.

He would look up at her, his face blank and innocent, a noticeable worry crease becoming further etched into his brow. "What love?" he would ask.

"The tapping of the spoon, you do it three times and then pause, then three times again. You haven't noticed it?" she would lower her voice, teasing him.

He would grin sheepishly knowing his mother's OCD tendencies (the woman could frequently be found at 4am with a toothbrush going to work on cleaning every crevice in the bathroom whenever insomnia struck) had snuck in again.

"Sorry babe," he'd say, his eyes beaming brightly, happy to

be distracted from whatever stress was getting in the way. "I suppose I'm a little stressed about this ridiculous story my editor is making me write – 11 kids with MIPs all on the same day between three different coastal towns. I mean, it's the Oregon Coast, this is what kids do here. How is this suddenly a story?" His brow would furrow again and she could tell he was back to overanalyzing and overthinking things. She had come over to him then, kissed his forehead right where that crease was making itself known and wrapped her arms around him. He nestled his head into her breasts, wrapping his arms tightly around her waist.

They lived a simple life in the small coastal town of Oceanside, Oregon – but it was theirs. They loved living so close to the ocean, Marcus' lame job notwithstanding. Allie worked at the local court house and had been there ever since she graduated college. She had met Marcus at a seaside farmers market after she and her college boyfriend parted ways. She would never forget that day. She was with her mom who was chatting away about the latest town gossip – there was always something happening in a small town that everyone was hell bent on discussing ad nauseam – when she saw him, when they saw each other really.

He was sampling homemade pies from Alice's Country House and while his mouth was full of delicious pie their eyes locked. They both laughed and smiled and then before she could stop herself, she walked right away from her mom (mid-gossip) and right over to him – her smile easy and wide.

"Hey there," Allie said slowly, her head tilting gently to one side. Her blue strapless maxi dress swaying lightly in the breeze.

"Hey to you," Marcus had responded in his boyish way, his blue eyes looking her up and down and taking her all in. He only appeared slightly out of place from the other country boys in his blue-striped Gap button-up, dark indigo jeans and brown Ecco loafers. He raised his full hands and offered, "Marionberry pie?"

"How did you know? Marionberry just so happens to be

my very favorite pie in the whole wide world. That's why I came over here actually," Allie teased, uncharacteristically flirtatious. It wasn't her style to approach a man, but with Marcus there hadn't even been a question, instinct and impulse led her. Led her right to her destiny, or so she had thought.

He was visiting from the nearest and largest city in Oregon – Portland – but after only a few months of long-distance dating he snagged a reporter gig for the local paper and they moved in together. And now, now after six years together and at breakfast no less, he wanted out.

"So, let me get this straight Marcus," Allie was attempting to locate her composure as she felt anger bubbling to the surface. Could this have really all be happening over a sales girl? "You've known for quote-un-quote awhile that our marriage wasn't working, but you decided that now, here at breakfast on a random Thursday was the perfect time to share this with me. Why the hell haven't you been talking to me about what's been going on? I can't imagine that this is a decision you made overnight. I've asked you for weeks what's been going on – I've noticed how distracted you've been. But rather than tell me ending our marriage was on your mind, you brushed it off as being tired or stressed."

Marcus grimaced. Surely he must have expected that she would want more details besides, "I don't want to be married anymore."

"It's not something we can talk our way through Allie. It's done for me, it's over. I knew that when I told you, you would want to try a variety of ways to work through it. But I'm past that point Allie, I really am."

She hated that he was using her name when he spoke. She used to love it, she used to ask him to say her name, especially when they made love. The way it rolled off his lips and into the air felt so right to her – as though he was the man who was destined to say her name. The first time he said it she knew he was the only man she ever wanted saying her name – in the bedroom, in the kitchen – anywhere. They were standing there, well, she was standing there while he ate that pie looking up at her so sweetly. "Allie. Well, it is an absolute pleasure to meet you Allie. Now, why don't you sit down and eat some pie with me?"

And in this moment, Allie would have done pretty much anything to get a pie into her hands. A juicy marionberry pie. A pie she could nonchalantly throw in his face, just as nonchalantly as he had ended their marriage.

Who does this? Allie wanted to know. Wasn't that what marriage and vows were about, a promise that couldn't be arbitrarily broken because one person decided they were "done"? She hesitated and considered asking about Stephanie, but she was too afraid. She realized in that moment that that she didn't want to know the truth; she really didn't want to know the full extent of the damage to their marriage, she only wanted to go lie down.

2

And lying down became most of what Allie did.

For the next year.

After Marcus left – and it hadn't taken him long – she holed up in their home, their coastal dream home which was now hers only making appearances at the courthouse for work and the grocery store for food – when she absolutely had to have it.

"Oh, honey you are way too thin, you've got to eat something," her mom chided her.

Allie would shrug. Apparently divorce was the best weight loss plan ever; it was unfortunate that she had been far too depressed to enjoy it. Allie knew how she was supposed to react. She had watched friends in the past go through divorce and immediately dive into the party scene, getting breast implants and spray tans and in general seeming to lose all sense of the power that women in their thirties truly possessed. And here she was, 31 and divorced. But, instead of joining her friends at the local dive bar to hang out, she could barely drag her ass – her now very tiny ass – to work. In fact, the thought of going out anywhere almost made her sick.

Her sisters had tried to inspire her into action as well, but Shelby and Laney were in Portland – about an hour and a half drive from where Allie lived at the beach and she could easily dodge them via phone, text and email. And they weren't as insistent as they might have been because Shelby was very close to giving birth to her first child with her partner Daniel. Laney was Shelby's main support (other than Daniel) and she was also very busy living in an eco-friendly co-housing community where her free spirited lifestyle kept her on the go. Laney also had a strong belief in the Law of Attraction – something Marcus had taught Allie about. According to it, the divorce was happening because it was either part of Allie's vibration, meaning somehow she had summoned it or it was divine timing that was working to her benefit. While she originally loved the concept of Law of Attraction, the notion that the divorce had been part of life "working out for her" was more than she could currently handle. She still believed that it was Marcus who had done this terrible thing to her – it had been Marcus who reneged on their plan, their plan of life together, of growing old with one another. She felt like the victim of a cruel joke played out by the Universe and talking to Laney about it felt like more energy and effort than she had to give.

Even so, her older sisters had tried to get her out of her divorce-coma (affectionately named as such by her sisters. Allie was too depressed to argue.). Shelby had invited her to numerous gatherings that she and her best friend Kathryn and Kathryn's husband Scott were throwing, but again, Allie felt repulsed by the thought of small talk and forced fun. Her other two sisters, Brittany and Alicia lived on the Coast near her, but since they were in their early 20's they were still in that young partying stage. Again, the thought of spending nights at dive bars potentially dating men she went to grade school with absolutely made Allie's stomach sour. Alicia and Brittany tried to woo her repeatedly, but since she was their big sister, they listened to her emphatic "no's".

Allie just couldn't rally herself into anything. Her body constantly hurt, she slept an inordinate amount of time and couldn't summon the energy to do much of anything. She felt a lot of sadness and fear when she let herself feel anything at all. Why did this happen to her? How had she managed to ruin her marriage? Some days her mind went in too many different directions making her feel crazy at best. She did what she could to manage it on her own and only succumbed to a three-way call or two from her well-meaning sisters when ignoring them also became too exhausting. Mostly, she found that she felt the most relieved when she was able to be alone, caring for her aching body to the best of her ability and staying away from unnecessary stimulation. Like conversation. At work, she kept things to pleasantries and got her job done but she was virtually unable to do anything above and beyond that. While some part of her knew she was depressed, another part of her felt like she was doing exactly what she needed to do to heal – just being present with her divorce-coma. She assumed some Zen Master somewhere could probably back her up on this.

She did, however, have one outlet that no Zen Master or man of any God would most likely approve of – her sudden divorce-coma option of choice – relentless television watching. With the TV on, she didn't feel so alone. And sometimes she even got herself into plank pose while watching Scandal or Housewives of (insert whatever city you prefer here) so it was almost like it was a positive influence. Almost. Most of the time she laid on the couch, dozing on and off, wondering when she was ever going to feel better. She did her best to avoid romantic movies of any kind, but one dreary Coastal Saturday she found herself watching Sex & the City – the movie – on TBS. She wanted to turn the channel. She knew she should. But the sparkles caught her attention. It had been so long since she had dressed up or gone out or had fun. She didn't know why but she found herself drawn in by Carrie Bradshaw's shiny shoes and then right there decided she was more of a Charlotte, with conservative and practical taste. But the sparkles had done their trick and now she couldn't stop watching…

An hour in and she was crying when Big drove away from the wedding, bawling when Carrie beat him over the head with her bouquet and downright undone when Charlotte screamed at Big while holding Carrie. They knew her pain. When Carrie looked at herself in the mirror after the debacle, Allie winced in pain. The raw pain etched deeply into her face, Allie knew she had looked about the same since the day Marcus left. She just couldn't get herself to do anything with her hair or her face or her clothes. She couldn't believe it. The girls of Sex & the City understood her pain.

Then, the darkness began to lift. Allie felt her heart expand while she watched Carrie color her hair a delicious, deep chocolate brown and totally redecorate her apartment and her wardrobe. She felt almost excited at the thought that perhaps she too could re-make herself, her life and rise above the pain she felt in her heart when Marcus made his breakfast announcement. Hope filtered in. Maybe it was possible for her to pull herself out of her divorce-coma sooner rather than later.

By the end of the film, true love back in place, fabulous clothes, sparkling heels and smooth tresses all in a state of perfection, Allie couldn't help but notice that she was sitting up on her couch, not lying down and certainly sitting up higher than she had been in the past year.

Without even thinking, she picked up her phone to call the one person she knew could help her with this.

"She lives! What up sis?" Brittany answered the phone in her usual buoyant tone.

"Haha, very funny. I need your help and I need you to keep it between you and me."

"Know something and not tell anyone about it? Not only would it be a family first, but I would love to be in on it. Who are we killing?!"

Brittany loved to tease and Allie couldn't help but crack a smile. She wasn't sure what had gotten in to her but she knew she had Sex & the City to thank for it.

———

"So...let me get this straight. You've been in your divorce-coma for almost a year now and it took Sex & the City – the movie – to get you out of it?" Brittany couldn't seem to hide her total enthrallment with this new turn in Allie's story as she gently washed Allie's hair. "Sex & the City and you suddenly realized that your roots were halfway down your head and you needed a totally new look?" Brittany shook her head in disbelief.

Allie smiled. It was true, her roots were about a year over due. Somehow seeing Carrie Bradshaw flip her hair back in gorgeous shiny wonder had snapped something within her.

"Yep, I guess so. It's literally like that movie flipped a light on inside of me. If Carrie can overcome a break up like that from Big, why can't I recover from Marcus?"

Brittany lifted Allie up and wrapped her head in a luxurious white towel. Then she leaned down to make eye contact with her sister.

"You do know that Carrie Bradshaw is a character in a movie and a TV series, not a real person, right?"

Allie rolled her eyes and stuck out her tongue.

"Oh, you're playful now too, huh? Did Carrie Bradshaw teach you that?" Brittany laughed back at her.

"Listen, I get that it seems silly to you, but you didn't go through a divorce, I did. I thought Marcus and I were going to be together forever. I wasn't prepared for him to walk out after 5 years," Allie explained as they walked back to Brittany's hair station at The Hair Universe. Her station was decked out in red, black and white – very dramatic and a little dark – but professional – just like Brittany.

Brittany softened as Allie said this. "I know sweetie, I really am only teasing you. I can't imagine what it would be like to have the person you thought you were going to spend your life with bail, at breakfast no less, randomly after 5 years of marriage. Although you know Laney and Shelby would tell you it wasn't random at all."

Allie sighed. "I know. And part of me now can feel that they might be right, but it's still too much for me to get a handle on just yet. I'm starting with the hair, baby steps for this girl."

Brittany smiled. "Hair make-over in full effect sis, by the time we finish you're gonna feel and look so good you'll be hotter than Carrie Bradshaw...or Charlotte – who you're more like."

Allie laughed out loud. "That's who I think I'm like too! Love it – now let's do this." The two sisters high-fived, Brittany poured Allie a glass of cheap white wine and the make-over began.

———

Allie walked out of Brittany's studio feeling more fantastic than she had before she had married Marcus. Brittany had given her a full and deep round of highlights, lighter at the face with darker pieces underneath to accentuate the lighter colors. She had cut her once blah shoulder length sandy brown hair to a dramatic A-line with the pieces in the front much longer than the stacked back. She worked with Allie's stick straight hair and smoothed it out with hair shine and a straightener.

Then, just for fun Brittany had done her make-up – showing her how to use eye liner and eye shadow, blush and bronzer. Allie couldn't believe it, she was like a new woman. When they finished, Brittany's eyes filled with tears.

"It's so good to see you looking so happy and radiant after so long Allie. He really did do you a favor by leaving. You deserve a man who loves you so much that he would never leave your side." Brittany had leaned in and given Allie a huge hug, squeezing her tight. It was then that Allie's eyes filled with tears too.

"I hope I can feel that way someday. Thank you, sis." Allie whispered to Brittany. Then she pulled back and wiped her eyes. "But in the meantime, at least I look fabulous!"

Allie felt so great, she felt like she should go somewhere, like she needed to be out with her new look. But she knew that her small town would instantly be abuzz with the news and it would quickly make its way back to sisters and mom. There was still more she needed to do before she unveiled the new

Allie to not only herself but her family. With that, she headed home to plot her next step.

———

Allie surveyed the scene of her home, of the home that she and Marcus had purchased together. It was gorgeous. Ocean view, open, wide spaces, minimally decorated in purples and blues and whites – colors that Marcus and she had picked out together. Everywhere she turned she saw Marcus and a memory of their life together. She shook her head. If she was ever going to get over the divorce, she was going to have to do something about the house.

"Like gut it completely," she said out loud.

She sighed as she walked through each of the small 3 bedrooms wondering what she could do to make the place feel less like the place she had lived in with her ex.

Before she knew it, she was on her phone again.

"Allie! Oh my god! You're calling me! This is so exciting!" Laney's high-pitched screams almost blew out Allie's ear drum.

"Good god Laney, yes, I'm calling you. Is it really scream-worthy?"

"Um, it's been almost a year since you have been willing to reach out to any of us, so yes, it's scream-worthy!" Laney said as she slowly raised the pitch of her voice again. This time Allie was prepared and pulled the phone far away from her ear.

"Okay, well could I convince you to talk in a more normal tone for the duration of the conversation?" Allie pleaded.

"Well, you're in luck because I'm on my way into Whole Foods, so I'll have to talk like a normal person now, although in my mind I'll still be screaming with excitement," Laney giggled.

Allie smiled. She really was so blessed that her sisters cared so much about her.

"Thank you, sweetie. Okay, you are probably wondering what would motivate me to call you after so long and I'm happy to tell you but I need you to keep this a secret from the other girls. I want to wait until I have some more pieces in place before I share with everyone. I know this is a stretch for our family – but can you do it and keep this conversation to yourself?"

"Pplllleeeaaaassssee, you know that the only ones who have trouble keeping secrets is Alicia and Shelby. I'm totally a safe person for you. Brittany does okay on secrets, but I'm still the best at keeping things tight-lipped. So, yes, whatever your secret is, it's totally safe with me. Have you decided to join the PeaceCorp? Track down Marcus's car and TP it? Go vegan?"

Now it was Allie laughing. "I hope that you do not think that any of those options would be the secret I have. Geez Laney."

Laney joined her in laughing. "Oh my god, Allie – you're laughing. Things really are shifting for you. So, spit it out, what's going on? I'm standing in front of the bulk foods which means you could lose my attention at any moment to a great deal on granola."

Allie rolled her eyes. Of course Laney was buying granola at Whole Foods. Knowing her it was likely hemp granola.

"Okay my hippie sista, I need your hippie help. This house. How can I live here when Marcus's energy is in every single thing? Do I completely gut the place? Sell it? Energetically how damaging is it for me to stay here?

This wasn't a conversation she could have with anyone else except for Laney and Shelby. But it was really Laney's area of expertise. She and her housemates had completely redecorated their entire house to Feng Shui energetic principles to encourage and support the highest vibrational frequency of their home. Laney frequently credited unexpected checks in the mail and hot dates to updates to the wealth and love corners of her room and home.

"Oh, thank god. I was praying we would have this conversation at some point. Overall, staying in the same home that you shared with your ex is not good Allie. I've often thought that being in that house was part of what was keeping you depressed. So, the first thing you need to do is sage the hell out of that place. Go down to that hole-in-the-wall woo-

woo bookstore on Main Street and they sell sage in the back of the store. Get a lot of it. When you get home, light it and go through every room in the house and to every corner of the house with it. You've got to begin releasing his energy from the space."

It occurred to Allie that maybe part of her inertia *was* feeling Marcus's energy and all of the heaviness from the break-up.

"Alright, I'm on it. Should I say anything as I move the sage smoke from room to room?"

"Yes, do! Say, "I now release anything not of the highest light from my home and I call in the highest vibration of love and light to fill every corner here." Or something like that. Essentially you want to release the negative and call in the highest light. I am so proud of you Allie. How did you know you needed to do something to your place?"

"It's sort of a long story but I will tell you that I got inspired and I walked into the house today and knew I had to change something. What do you think about me bringing in someone to do Feng Shui in here? Is that worth it? Or should I just sell the whole thing?"

Allie wasn't sure why but selling the house kept popping in as an option. She felt so disgusted with Marcus and the energy she had been sitting in the thought of staying there any longer made her feel sick.

"Well, if you remember Allie, you were the one who fell in love with the house. Remember how Marcus said he would do it for you and that it wasn't his favorite but that if you really wanted it, you two could get it? I think it's meant to be your house but we need to get Marcus's energy out of there. So start with saging the hell out of the place – sage every day for a week and then once a week or more after that. Open all of the windows as you sage too. I can also give you the information of the Feng Shui consultant we worked with. Her name is Christine and she is divine. Totally spiritually tuned in and can support you in creating a home that will truly be yours and will be primed for abundance to flow to you in many ways."

"Wow, somehow I had forgotten that Marcus wasn't as in love with the house as I was. So saging is on, text me your Feng Shui lady's info after we get off the phone and I'll contact her. Maybe there is some way to save this house and make it truly my own."

"Allie – I'm so happy to hear from you. And I am so happy that you are feeling ready to make some changes so you can experience all of the joy life has to offer you. Marcus really did give you a gift by setting you free, I promise." Laney almost whispered as she spoke these last words.

Allie felt tears fill her eyes. A gift in divorce? Allie shook her head. She knew Laney meant well but she just couldn't see it. In the meantime, though, she had to do something about the house and looking down at her outfit – old Levi's and a crew neck orange tee – something about her clothes.

"Thank you Laney. Someday I hope I believe you. I'll keep you posted on what happens with Christine and the house, and remember – don't tell anyone."

"You've got my word sista," Laney said with love in her voice. "I love you."

"Love you too Lane – thank you again!"

When they hung up, Allie surveyed her large living room, bookcase, huge windows looking out at the ocean. She imagined putting everything up for sale and replacing all of it. Instinctively she began to pull out books from the bookshelf that were not truly her taste, but had been books Marcus had enjoyed or forgotten to take with him when he moved out. She put them in a box and when she was done with that, she dug into her closets to remove anything that made her think of or remember Marcus.

She was on her way to clearing him right out of her energy field. Allie had to chuckle. Laney and Shelby would sure love to hear her say those words. Energy field. Who did she think she was anyway? Some spiritual guru??

———

Allie surveyed the scene and loved what she saw. She ran her fingers through her freshly cut and brilliantly blonde hair and relaxed her hands on her hips. Her home felt like hers again. She had saged it every day for a week and would continue as instructed by Laney, at least once a week regularly. She had also gotten rid of anything that was even mildly associated with Marcus, and already she felt better than she had felt in a year. Her living space overlooking the ocean was now simplified; a big cushy rug she impulsively purchased from the local furniture store Roby's, her white couch, two sitting chairs and a book case. It felt clean, it felt free – just like how Allie was beginning to feel. Her dining room contained her table and one large painting that she felt suited her, one Shelby had gotten her years ago but which she hadn't hung up because Marcus thought it was too "cheesy". It said "Love is Spoken Here." Allie loved it.

She had gotten rid of extraneous kitchen appliances and loved all of the open counter space that was now hers. Her bedroom was also uber simplified. She got rid of the king bed she and Marcus had shared and bought herself a queen pillow top with a decadent, silky purple comforter and red and purple throw pillows. She tossed their night stands too and replaced it with a small, pine alter-style corner bookcase, a large white armoire and wicker basket for her books. It was finally her room – with no sign of Marcus anywhere to be found.

The his and her sinks in the bathroom even got their own make-over. Allie spread all of her bathroom goods to both sides and bought new hand soap for each sink. She was having fun alternating washing her hands at either sink, reclaiming that space for herself as well.

Allie hadn't felt this clear since Marcus left and she didn't want the transformation to end. She looked down at her plaid button up, oversized shirt with jean capris and tennis shoes and laughed. Next up to her return from the divorce-coma was going to have to be her wardrobe. One of the things that struck her when she got pulled into the Sex & the City movie vortex, was how fabulous the ladies dressed. They really took care of themselves and wore clothes that seemed to perfectly convey their mood and their fabulousness. Allie had always been one to dress for comfort, she had been shopping at the Gap for as long as she could remember. And it was time for all of that to change. Starting today.

———

"Wait – shut up – you are here, right now, in Portland?" the disbelief in Shelby's voice was impossible to mask. She hadn't known her sister Allie to do anything spontaneously, in well, forever.

Allie laughed. "I know it's highly unlike me to just up and drive into the city, without planning ahead of time and calling you and Laney, but this is serious business and I need my big sister's support."

"Well, you know you've got it. Me and my big baby belly will meet you wherever you want us to."

"Hmm…that's sort of the thing, Shelb. I need to totally redo my wardrobe but I've been shopping at the Gap for so long I have no idea where to go. I thought maybe since you're about 5000 times more hip than me you might be able to help. I think Laney would tell me to get hemp clothing and that's not exactly the look I'm going for." Allie loved Laney's laid back, hippie style but it wasn't what was calling her. After years of basic Gap apparel, she was ready to sex things up a bit.

"Okay, I'm on it Allie. We are going to find you some sexy clothes for your big return. Let's meet at Pioneer Place in downtown in half an hour. They've got Bebe, H&M, BCBGMAXAZRIA, and J.Crew. Plus, a Victoria's Secret. It will be the perfect mix. And Allie… is this something we are telling the girls about or are you keeping your makeover on the down-low? I'm gonna suggest keeping it quiet and then a big reveal to everyone," Shelby concluded breezily, as she was most comfortable in big sister save the day mode.

Allie giggled. "And this is why I called you. Yes, we are keeping things on the DL and yes to everything else you said. I'm so excited to see what we find!"

It wasn't lost on Allie that she had contacted almost all of her sisters for help in her return all the while telling each of them to keep it under wraps. She wondered if they would be able to and then realized she didn't really care anymore.

She was finally beginning to feel like herself, her true self, a self she had not been aware of during her years with Marcus.

———

"That is simply too good not to buy," Shelby exclaimed as Allie turned this way and that while donning a BCBG emerald green dress with a slit so high she was afraid she would have to wear black hip-hugger panties so as to keep from flashing everyone. Even so it was exquisite and fit her like a glove.

"I have no idea where I would ever wear it," Allie said as she turned to view the back. "But you're right, I cannot say no to it," she said as she smoothed the front of the dress as it hugged her breasts and waist perfectly.

Shelby was sitting on a cushy couch outside the dressing room.

"3 stores and a new wardrobe later…How are you feeling Allie? Dropping all of this cash making you nervous? You are not messing around today sister, I'm in awe of you. It's like a switch was flipped and you're back and better than ever."

Allie smiled, as she tucked a strand of blonde hair behind her ear looking around at the bags and piles of clothes around her. BCBG was the place for the sexy dresses, she had grabbed up some pretty and sensual sleepwear at Vicky's Secret, along with some playful workout clothes from the Pink line, H&M had given her a whole new sassy work wardrobe, with a few pieces sprinkled in from Forever 21. Coach had been all about the shoes and a fabulous leather handbag. Allie couldn't believe it. This was the new, upgraded her. And it felt so good. The money she was spending didn't faze her one bit.

"You know Shelby, I never told anyone, not even Marcus, but I spent years squirreling away money, thinking that for our 10-year anniversary Marcus and I would have a destination vow renewal and fabulous vacation – something we didn't have the first time around. After he left I thought about using it to pay off a huge chunk of the house, but ... something clicked and it all changed for me. I decided that spending the money on myself would be the best investment I could make."

Shelby was so inspired that she hoisted herself up and waddled over to Allie to high-five and then hug her. Tears filled her eyes as she hugged Allie. "You did it girl, you did it. You're now officially on the other side of the divorce-coma." She pulled back to look at Allie. "I knew this whole thing was leading you to something bigger and better and looks like you are getting it started baby girl." With that Shelby kissed Allie on the forehead.

Tears filled Allie's eyes. She felt the power of Shelby's words. She had never felt so clear and free in her life. And while she wasn't 100 percent recovered from the heartbreak of Marcus leaving, she was damn near close. Shelby's words echoed in her mind as she contemplated the possibility that Marcus leaving her was to set her free into more of who-she-really-was.

———

With a bright and shiny new haircut and color, a cleansed home in every sense of the word and a closet full of vibrant clothes, high heels and cashmere/silk blends – Allie felt like a new woman.

She woke up the Saturday following her impromptu weekend shopping trip in Portland to a beautiful April morning at the coast with sunlight streaming in through her curtains the sound of the ocean melodically roaring in the background. Somehow she knew then that she was through the worst of it. Marcus was gone. Long gone. The divorce was final. Allie was here and she was not going to leave herself, she was going to stay and enjoy this life one way or the other. She was surprised to notice that phrases from the Law of Attraction work of Abraham-Hicks began popping into her head that sunny morning and then all day long in email and in conversations – seemingly all around her. Something in what Shelby had said to her had stuck. That somehow this was all happening *for* her. She knew with an unprecedented certainty that she needed to find a way to get to happy and then let the Universe have its way with her from there. She had so much life to live, she couldn't let a man leaving her end it all. Even if it had been Marcus. Even if it had been the man she thought she was going to spend the rest of her life with.

That sunny spring day marked the "return of Allie" as her mother and sisters began to call it. She had text her mom to see about meeting at the farmer's market and noticed quite excitedly that she didn't feel an ounce of dread. She was going to be okay. It was as if her soul had done the grieving it needed to and now she was being called forth into the next chapter of her life.

Her mom had rallied the troops, and when Allie arrived at the market she was met by her sisters Brittany and Alicia as well as her mom and stepdad Bob. Bob and her mom had been together for what seemed like forever, but was really more like 20-something years. Their dad had left long ago when they were all very little. He and their mom had married super young and his drinking and partying ways had taken precedence over his duties as a father. Bob had had a rough start coming into a family of 5 girls, but over time he gained their trust and was now a part of their family that they all deeply loved.

Allie felt like she sparkled. She was wearing a cute, yet sexy aqua blue halter dress from Victoria's Secret (thanks semi-annual sale!) along with wedge sandals from Coach. Her blonde locks were smoothed out and she swore she felt a bounce in her step when she walked.

"Oh honey, you're back! And you look gorrrggeeeooouuusss!" her mom squealed with delight as she extended her arms out for a hug, noticeably eyeing Allie up and down with approval. "We didn't know if you would ever come out of your funk. But I have been praying for you and I knew some day the Lord would give you the strength to join the land of the living again." She squeezed Allie tight. Allie looked over at Brittany and Alicia who were smiling brightly and once sister eye contact was made they all rolled their eyes in unison. Her mom meant well, but after the divorce from their dad so many years ago, she had become overly active in a local Christian church and was always praying for someone. Although after her marriage to their dad, it was understandable that she would seek solace in religion and in the arms of one of her dad's former hunting buddies, Bob. The topic of her mom's zealous beliefs were ignored by all and simply tolerated because the girls loved her too much to say more than, "Mom, pllleeeeasssse." Fortunately, that was usually enough to quiet her right down.

"And anyway," her mom whispered as she held onto Allie. "None of us really liked Marcus. You were too good for him."

"Okay mom, enough," Alicia came in to break up the hug fest that was now turning into a suffocating grip. Alicia turned to face her mother, her strawberry red curls piled high on top of her head. "Remember what we told you, there will be no mention of his name – ever again by any of us." She nodded over at Brittany who smiled in support and put her arm around Allie. "We are a team. If a man fucks with one of us, he fucks with all of us." She pointed over at Bob. "So Bob, take note of that. Now, Allie, welcome back! We missed you and there is *a lot* we need to catch you up on." With that Alicia looped her arm through Allie's and grabbed Brittany as they led her through the farmer's market. Allie was impressed, not only were her sisters incredibly committed to having her back, it seemed Brittany and the other girls had not leaked word of Allie's transformation to one another

"Just so you know Allie, we weren't really all that worried about you," Brittany winked. "And I mean that in a good way. We knew you were processing what happened. Sorry mom was so dramatic, but you know how she is. I told her several times to leave you alone and that you would contact us when you were ready. And sorry about my numerous drunk texts last week for you to join us at the Upper Deck. We just missed you, but we weren't worried!" She laid her head on Allie's shoulder. "By the way, fabulous hair! You have a new secret stylist?"

21

Allie reached over and mused Brittany's tight curly black locks, giving her a quick kiss on the forehead and smiling back at her. "Yeah, one Miss Brittany. Seriously girl, you did the most amazing job." Alicia looked over at them, narrowing her gaze.

"What?! You saw Brittany to get your hair done and you two didn't tell me?? And where did you get such fabulous clothes? Wait a minute...did Shelby take you shopping??" Alicia was half-joking and half-serious. Spending sister time together without informing the others was a clear violation of sister code. One Allie knew she had repeatedly violated over the past 2 months, but she knew her sisters would understand that she needed time to ease back into her life.

Allie leaned in and put her arm around Alicia too. "Sweetie, I had to ease my way back into the land of the living and if I told all of you that I was starting to feel half-human again, I knew it would be too much energy to manage. I had to go slow. So yes, Brittany did my hair." Allie looked over at Brittany. "Big ups to you baby sis for not blabbing our hair time to everyone."

"I told you I could keep a secret!" Brittany swatted playfully over at Alicia, loving the opportunity to be in on something that she wasn't.

"Energy? Too much energy to manage? Oh my god Allie, did you spend time with Laney too? You're killing me here," Alicia actually looked concerned that her sister was transforming right before her eyes.

Allie and Brittany laughed. "Well, I did have a Feng Shui, energy consultation with Laney's support, yes. But that wasn't actual in person time, just phone time. You know, Lish, you might want to check out this energy thing, there seems to be something to it."

Alicia rolled her eyes and Allie kissed her on the cheek. "I love you, girl, don't be mad at me. Celebrate with me!"

Alicia cracked a smile and stopped, turning to face Allie, looking her up and down. "You do look better than I've ever seen you. Nice work Britt!" Alicia reached over to high-five her sister. "And we've got to give Shelby props for however she convinced you to reform your wardrobe. I've been nagging at you for years. Just promise me that soon, very soon, you'll let me be in on a secret none of the other girls will be in on?"

Brittany circled around, linking her arm with Allie's and then Alicia's.

"Okay, deal. Thank you for understanding, Lish. And Britt, just to clarify about your little comment earlier – I was around for *some* stuff this year; I did show up to birthdays and the holiday stuff. But I know, that was about it, other than the makeover you very successfully helped me with."

"C'mon Allie," Alicia chimed in. "Even when you were there, you weren't really there. You know what we mean. Either way, we're really happy you're back with us! Like really, really back. Like damn girl, you look hot. You actually have color on your face and a little kick in your step," Alicia said as she swatted Allie's behind. "We like having our Allie back."

They walked right by Alice's Country House booth and Allie smiled as she noticed she didn't feel sad or even angry at the thought of Marcus. Somehow it all felt so long ago, she could feel the sweetness of that moment combined with the knowing that it was over and nothing more needed to be felt or addressed when it came to him. It no doubt helped that she had her two younger sisters with her. Their support always made her feel stronger – when she allowed it to. She felt so blessed to be with her girls and no longer be caught in her "divorce-coma." The girls ran up ahead to their favorite crepe stand while Allie surveyed the scene.

Brittany was the youngest of the five girls and like their mother had dark curly hair, fair skin and beautifully clear sky blue eyes. She was a pleaser, always willing to go along with whatever the other sisters were up to, although in the past few years she had begun taking a stand and speaking her mind. This was new for all of them, but Allie knew an important part of Brittany's maturing process. Alicia was the ginger of the five girls with beaming cheeks, bewitching green eyes and strawberry blonde curls that went on forever. She loved to party, managed a local drive-through espresso stand and seemed totally content to live her life in this way for as long as she desired. Allie signed. She so loved these girls, she was grateful they gave her the space for her divorce-coma and she was grateful they were here to cheer on her return to active living. Spending this time with them also made her heart ache for her other two sisters Shelby and Laney.

"Well, I'll be damned. If it isn't Miss Allie Strauss." A voice boomed from behind taking her out of the moment. She spun around to see no other than her best guy friend from high school Neil Willis.

"Neil! I haven't seen you in a thousand years. How the hell are you?"

"Better now," he replied as he scooped her up giving her a huge hug. "What are you up to these days, lady?"

"Oh you know, living the dream – working at the courthouse, enjoying the small town life, I've got a great house with an ocean view and that keeps me pretty happy. What about you?" Allie carefully omitted the parts of her life that involved divorce and spending the past year in survival mode. Besides, she was starting over fresh and she didn't need to stay stuck in the past by talking about it. She vaguely remembered from her time studying the Law of Attraction that talking about what one didn't want kept it active – not a place she wanted to be right this moment – that was for sure.

Neil put his hand on Allie's shoulder and gave it a little squeeze. "I heard about Marcus leaving, I'm so sorry Allie. It must have been a really tough time."

Allie did everything she could not to allow tears to fill her eyes. Of course Neil knew, of course everyone on the entire coastline knew or anyone connected to anyone on the coast for that matter. That was the way small towns operated. How could Allie have forgotten? She managed a strained smile.

"Actually Neil, no need to be sorry – I am finally feeling better about things. I mean who knows, maybe one day the divorce will be the best thing that ever happened to me?" Allie really wanted to keep the conversation light. She had always found Neil sort of cute and the years since high school had been good to him. The last thing she wanted was him feeling sorry for her.

"Oh, I'm so happy to hear that Allie. You're just the sweetest girl and I know how much being married meant to you. You've got the right attitude, that's for sure."

Neil did seem genuinely happy for her, but Allie couldn't help but feel a bit of a sting in his words. In high school she had a distinct fantasy about her husband and marriage and the family they would create. She remembered Neil and her talking about their future families back in the day, with her wondering at that time if perhaps her future could be with him. Allie had always been a bit wistful and romantic. Obviously Neil remembered this about her.

"So anyway, let's get to the good stuff. What are you up to these days? I haven't seen you around here in forever."

Allie honestly hadn't seen much of Neil since high school graduation. They had intersected at various points along the way – a party here, during the holidays, etc. – but nothing substantial enough to warrant a deeper conversation. Obviously Neil's mother Edna had filled him in on her marital activities. She wondered what else Neil knew about her. She batted this thought away, it didn't matter and it wasn't like she was going to date her high school best friend at the age of 31. Although, his tanned arms and strong hands were definitely catching her attention.

"Yeah, I'm still living in Portland and I'm working as an electrician. I love it. And actually I've got some really big news – I just met the girl I'm going to marry. Can you imagine that? Me married? We met at a Hollywood Bowl night a few months ago and have been together ever since. Her name is Becky. She's here somewhere." Neil turned around to try to spot her. "I'm not sure where but I would love for you to meet her. My mom took her to look at some cedar benches or something. You know girls, she is already redecorating my place, including my patio." Neil chuckled and Allie could see how proud he was to have met the woman that he would spend his life with.

In fact, Allie had never seen Neil's face light up like that –
even in high school – a time when life was fresh with
possibility. She did her best to smile. His marriage was getting
started when hers had ended. She had been feeling so good
today, how could she have thought it was going to last? How
could she have checked Neil out? *Ugh*, Allie thought to herself.
I'm a hot mess. Not only was she divorced, she was divorced at
age 31 – a time she should have been like Neil, excited to
spend her life with one person. Even so, Allie was not about
to let this incident – that she was not sure how she attracted
nor did she want to indulge that analysis just yet – take from
her ability to be a kind human being.

"That is so awesome Neil, I'm really happy for you. And
yes, I can imagine you married. She's a lucky girl." Allie did her
best to convey her feelings and leave her own self-judgment
and unworthy feelings out of the exchange. It wasn't Neil's
fault she couldn't keep a husband. Allie wished she could
magically transport herself somewhere else. Just then she
remembered something important.

"Hey Neil – how is your sister doing? Is she still living in
the Gulf of Mexico, in that little seaside town of Shorespoint?"

"Oh yeah, Tawna is doing great. She is living the life down
there, working for a bank, going out every night, meeting
tourists and has crazy stories to tell us every time she calls or
texts as that seems to be her preferred form of
communication. You guys don't stay in touch anymore?"

"Gosh, I haven't seen her since college and I think maybe
awhile back we Facebooked, but I haven't been on there in
forever. I do remember that even back then she had some
amazingly good stories to tell. Do you have her updated
contact information by chance?"

Before Allie knew it, she had Tawna's phone number and
email address, and a way to transport herself somewhere else
right away.

3

It didn't take long for Tawna to respond. Ever since seeing Neil at the market, Allie knew exactly what she needed to fully leave any post-marriage blahs behind. She needed a vacation somewhere sunny, warm and far away from where people knew anything about her.

Dear Allie,

OMG! It is soooo awesome to hear from you! Neil had text me the other day to say you might be contacting me. I'm so glad you did!

Girl, we gotta get you down here. You mentioned you might be up for visiting? Well, you totally should. There's this kick-ass strip down here (nothing like the "strip of Hwy 101 on the Coast of course!) called The Block filled with amazing bars, people and food. I have a studio apartment overlooking the ocean and even though it's small, you're totally welcome to stay. It will be cozy! I'm close to pretty much everything, so book your ticket, come stay with me and then – no worries – you can do your own thing and I'll do mine. Then, we can meet up whenever we both feel like it!

Sound good? If so, let's do this!

Love,

xoxoTawna

Allie wasn't entirely surprised by Tawna's response; it seemed not too much had changed from their college days.

Tawna had always been the life of the party – fun, a gorgeous blonde bombshell with one of those to-die-for voluptuous bodies that men fell all over themselves for. A long weekend in a new spot with the warm ocean, a free place to stay and time to do whatever she wanted sounded perfect. And then if she did get into the party mood, she would just have to call up…er…text Tawna.

Tawna was also a known man-magnet, no matter where they went or what they did back in college, Tawna was always known to snag a new guy. Allie had always felt like she was along for the ride with Tawna – she wasn't one to snag men as easily. She was much more reserved and shy, and typically met her boyfriends in study groups, not parties or being out on the town. She enjoyed Tawna's energy and it never bothered her that Tawna was always meeting or hooking up with someone new. She loved the stories and enjoyed the gossip. There were always some really, really good stories filled with plenty of drama and action and at least back in college, Allie had enjoyed her role with Tawna and all of the stories.

Allie remembered Tawna's college days of letting the good men, who adored her and treated her like a queen go, and settling instead on more dramatic relationships that ended up draining the life of both parties and usually culminating in a trauma-drama break-up of some sort. Sometimes police were called or hospital visits were made. Tawna's crazy antics had never directly impacted Allie and so she was happy to cheer her on from the side, trusting that at some point Tawna would figure it out. If there was any figuring out that was needed. Some ladies were meant for the man spotlight and some friends like Allie preferred to cheer their friends on from the side.

So, suffice it to say, Allie was anything but surprised when Neil seemed to hint that Tawna was still working the scene and the men. And while the thought of being Tawna's sidekick again didn't appeal to Allie, was more than relieved when Tawna suggested they meet up "whenever" as opposed to being obligated to spend every minute together. That was exactly the kind of vacation and life that Allie longed for – one filled with plenty of freedom.

It was like a gift from the Universe, she couldn't believe how easy it all had fallen into place. After receiving Tawna's email Allie went to Kayak.com and immediately found a great deal on airfare three weeks away. She forwarded Tawna her travel plan and got an immediate, "Woohoo!" reply along with the offer to pick her up from the airport so she didn't have to rent a car. Allie was excited. Her first vacation since the break-up and right at the perfect time – a time where she could get away, be by herself and have some celebration time.

Her co-workers and boss had almost a similar response to the end of her "divorce-coma" as her mom and sisters, and were more than thrilled when she announced she would be taking a few days off work to celebrate her return back to the land of the living. It was like she was riding a new wave of love and inspiration after spending a year in darkness. Allie couldn't believe their enthusiasm for her vacation and new lease on life. They even had flowers delivered to her the next day after her announcement in their team meeting, along with this thought-provoking card:

To Allie – Welcome back from the dark and into the light! We love you so much and will always be here for you! Love, Your Work Family Xo

Out of the dark and into the light, Allie whispered to herself, her thumb brushing over the embossing of the balloons on the small card. She sat back in her chair, leaning all of the way back propping her legs up on her desk. The phrase seemed to trigger a memory…

It was around 9p and Marcus still wasn't home. Allie was curled up in bed, her tortoise shell brown framed glasses on, her favorite Emily Giffin book in hand. She had always been a sucker for a good romance novel and with Marcus working later and later hours she was quickly making her way through all of Emily's books. Her phone had lighted up and beeped with an email from Marcus. She was happily surprised to hear from him at this hour, lately he hadn't messaged her to let her know what time he would be home. Instead of a message with his return, he had sent her an email with a link to an article, along with a note "Thought you might enjoy this. XoM

When she clicked on the link it took her to an article about Kundalini Awakenings and Dark Nights of the Soul. This was a few months before their breakfast break-up Allie realized. In hindsight, she wondered if he was trying to prepare her for what was coming. Allie immediately leaned forward and opened up her email. She knew that link would still be in her Trash folder at the very least. She searched "Marcus" in her Trash folder and the emails popped up. She did a quick scan from the bottom up and winced a little at the sight of "I love you" in the subject line of an email 6 months prior to their breakfast break-up. She shook it off and continued to scan up the list. Fortunately, it didn't take long for her find the email from about 1 month before the breakup on Kundalini Awakenings and Dark Nights of the Soul. Allie jumped right into the article, eating up the content in a way that she hadn't when Marcus had first sent the link. She had only assumed it was something new he was learning about that he wanted to share with her, not that she could potentially be on her way to such an intense awakening in her life.

As Allie read on, she absorbed the information on every level of her body-mind-Spirit, as she began to piece together what had occurred for her. Apparently, during these "awakenings" individuals are thrust into some sort of tragedy (and your husband of five years promptly ending your marriage over breakfast seemed to warrant this) that culminated in a time of deep darkness and angst. Allegedly all of this occurred so that the individual could become more of who they really were at the soul level. She had certainly spent the last year in darkness. Upon further investigation, she learned that often individuals who are going through this time felt as though they are going crazy (she had experienced many of those moments) as every aspect of who they thought they were was stripped away. They often had bizarre physical ailments that were diagnosed as "mystery" illnesses by traditional doctors.

Allie had experienced all of this. The past year had yielded to her chronic back pain, caused by seemingly nothing – no injury or explanation for it. She had also had a chronic sore throat for the first few months after Marcus left, again with no known medical cause and of which responded to zero medications or treatments. Laney and Shelby had three-way called her, explaining that her throat was her fifth chakra and that what her body was asking was for her to speak her truth. There were things she was not saying that she needed to say. And that her back was alerting her to the fact that she currently felt unsupported and as though all of her foundations had been removed from her life.

Allie couldn't argue with them so when they instructed her to do a journaling exercise of writing a letter to Marcus saying all of the things she never said but wanted to and then as a ritual burning it (after reading it out loud that was), she had no choice but to do it. Her sore throat dissolved within a week after that. Her back had been trickier to treat, and Shelby practically commanded her to have a BodyTalk session which was a form of energy medicine. Allie had instead tried every type of deep tissue remedy available – heating pads, cold packs, icy hot, massage – but all with no luck. It seems that in a Dark Night of the Soul/Kundalini Awakening physical ailments don't respond to traditional treatments because at this point the individual is no longer able to look at life from merely a physical perspective. Once this occurs, the emotional and spiritual aspects behind all physical ailments must be addressed in order for the body to heal fully.

Emotionally, Allie had thought she was Marcus's wife. She thought they were a team, a unit that was going to be together until the end of this life. Now she was being forced (thanks to Marcus) to discover herself in a completely new way. The vows were broken, the marriage over and now after a year of crying, and oscillating from being filled with rage and hatred to lethargic, Allie was ready to make sense of things. She wanted to feel good again. And perhaps what she was experiencing really was a spiritual awakening and not some indication that she sucked as a wife or had done something terribly wrong to bring this pain upon herself. That thought definitely made her whole body breathe a sigh of relief. She closed her eyes, still relaxed in her office chair – she really was going to be okay.

Her thoughts continued as she remembered that once a cycle of this awakening completed, an individual would wake up one day and feel totally different. The darkness would lift as the cycle of transformation they were in resolved. They were now a whole layer or many layers free of the old self and were more of who-they-really-were at the soul level. And Allie certainly felt exactly this way. Could it be she wondered? Could the divorce have been a Kundalini Awakening? There were no two better people to ask than her spiritually grounded sisters Shelby and Laney. Sure, she had dodged them repeatedly during her divorce-coma, but she knew that ultimately they understood that she was often a solo-processor. Shelby was the oldest of the five and always seemed to know the best next steps to take, and Laney had been involved in the new thought community for a long time and always provided an interesting perspective. Allie smirked to herself, finally it was her turn to demand a three-way call. Not surprisingly, her sisters jumped right at the chance and within a half hour they were all on the phone together.

"So ladies, you are probably wondering why I arranged this three-way call with you."

"Well actually, mom text us from the farmer's market a couple of weeks ago, so we had a feeling we might hear from you soon," Shelby excitedly responded.

"Good lord, can that woman keep anything to herself?" Allie moaned.

"I believe that's what we would call a redundant question," Laney quipped.

"You know mom, she loves a good story and for the past year it's all been about how much she hates Marcus and how worried she was about you. She was super excited to see a new chapter in the story emerge. That's all. Besides it's not like she text the whole family," Shelby remarked.

Laney cleared her throat loudly.

"What the f?" Allie jumped in. "Really, she told grandma and Lori too?" Their mother had been reporting their periods, boyfriends, break-ups, poor grade averages and everything in between to her mom (the girls' grandma) and her older sister for as long as they could remember.

"C'mon Allie, you can't be surprised," Laney scolded.

"No, no, you're right. I think I keep expecting her to grow out of the gossip phase." All three sisters laughed. "*Anyway*, so yes, I have arisen from my divorce-coma. But as I've been sorting through the details of it, it's come to my attention that perhaps what I was really going through was or is a Kundalini Awakening."

Laney and Shelby gasped in unison.

"Oh my god Allie, yes! Yes, yes!" Shelby squealed into the phone.

"Did I call this or did I call it, Shelb?" Laney retorted.

"What Laney – you knew?" Allie said.

"Well, I won't say I knew per se, but at some point along the way I did say to Shelby that Marcus was undoubtedly giving you a gift and that you were going to have to go through your dark night of the soul one way or the other – everyone has to. But I knew with utter confidence that you would then re-emerge more of who you really are – like everyone does – and even more so than you ever were or could be with him. So yeah, like a spiritual or Kundalini Awakening. I think folks are calling it a Spiritual Transformation or Spiritual Awakening these days." Laney explained with exacting detail.

"That is so crazy Laney because Marcus *sent me* an article on Kundalini cycles and Dark Nights of the Soul a month before the breakfast break-up. And then I woke up that Saturday morning and was like, 'Okay, I'm good now.' I mean, it's not like I don't have any pain around what happened, but it's not like this heavy weight on my soul, taking my breath away like it was for so long. Then to top everything off, my coworkers sent me flowers and the card said something about 'out of the dark and into the light' and suddenly I remembered the article. That's when I knew I had to pull you and Shelby in on the case."

"Do you think he was alerting you to what was about to happen? Sort of like he knew this was his role in your life story?" Shelby interrupted. "I mean on a deeply subconscious level, that is."

"You know, it did occur to me, like some part of him knew that ending the marriage was going to thrust me into a dark night of the soul and he was trying to prepare me in some way. It's just too bad I had no indication or knowledge that that's what was happening over the past year. Although, it has been really comforting to look back at what happened and where I am now and see the correlation. I literally feel like a different person, but it's almost like I don't recognize who she is yet, even though it's me. I don't know. Is any of this making any sense?"

"It's making perfect sense Allie," Laney and Shelby said in unison and then laughed.

"Really, it is. And we are so proud of you for putting these pieces together. It's like your awareness and consciousness is at a whole new level," Shelby said.

"Thank you girls, there was no way I could talk to Brittany or Alicia about this and certainly not mom. I'm excited to see what this transformation or awakening or whatever this is, is going to lead me to next. Which is why I've decided to go visit an old friend in the Gulf of Mexico next week for five days to get away, relax and get to know this new version of myself."

"Awesome! Who's the friend?" Laney asked.

"Tawna Willis, she's Neil's sister from high school. Remember Neil? He was my bestie in high school and then me and Tawna ended up hanging out for a while during college. She's offered to let me crash at her place and come and go as I please. I ran into Neil the other day at the market, at my first big outing as you already heard about. He was just so lit up about this girl he is going to marry and I stood there feeling like a complete loser. It dawned on me that he has a really fun sister who lives somewhere really fun. It seemed like a sign from the Universe to get away and press the resct button so I can handle perfectly normal conversations like the one with Neil that put me in a bit of an "I suck" spin cycle."

"Oh sweetie, you don't suck," Shelby interjected.

"Yeah, what Shelb said," Laney jumped in. "But I don't know Allie, maybe you should get your own hotel or Airbnb place instead of staying with her since you haven't spent time with her in so long? You both are probably really different people now. And after what you've been through, you are going to be really sensitive to energy. I remember Tawna being a really big personality and that might be too much for you right now."

"Oh Laney, leave her be. She's following the flow. Sign from the Universe? Kundalini Awakening? Dark night of the soul? Oh honey, welcome to our world!" Shelby giggled. "I can't wait to tell Kathryn about this, she is going to be so excited for you too."

Before long they realized it had been over two hours on the phone and Shelby was tired (she was 6 months along with her first child after all and Daniel was calling her for dinner) and Laney had to get to her community dinner since she was in charge of dessert for the meal. Kisses were blown into the phone and the girls said their good-byes. Allie hung up and realized she was still smiling. What if Laney was right and Marcus wasn't a shitty husband, but actually an angel who had set her free to have an even better life experience than she could have ever imagined?

4

"Flight 308 to Houston is now boarding."

Allie checked her ticket for the thousandth time and felt her stomach tighten. A few days ago she started feeling a sense of dread whenever she thought about taking the trip to Shorespoint. Tawna, while at first had been in regular communication and very helpful, had in recent days virtually stopped responding to Allie's emails after announcing she had met a new guy who she was sure was "the One." Allie couldn't help but wonder if it might be better for her to rent a car and get a hotel with an ocean view instead of counting on Tawna. Just because they had known one another for years and had been good friends at one time didn't mean she should expect her to be her airport chauffeur and hotel.

Allie had even considered canceling the trip, but with her coworkers and family cheering her on and her strong desire to wash that conversation with Neil out of her psyche, Allie kept brushing the "cancel, cancel" feelings aside. She could always get a hotel room if things with Tawna didn't work out, what was important was that she took time to relax and have a new experience outside of her usual comfort zone.

Since coming out of her divorce-coma or Kundalini Awakening or whatever it was she went through, she had been saging her home daily (courtesy of Shelby and Laney's mutual recommendation) to free the space of her depressive energy over the past year, not to mention the breakfast break-up aftermath. Sage was used in native traditions for its energetic cleansing properties and nowadays one could find it at any health food store or metaphysical bookstore. Fortunately, Allie had her sisters who shipped her enough sage wands to last her another year. As instructed by Laney, Allie would go to each corner of the house and ask that all negative energy be dissipated and that only energy of the highest love and light be in her space. She could feel a greater and greater lightness in her home with each saging. So, she brought some along with her for Tawna's…just in case this feeling of angst in her stomach was really her intuition signaling something more. She didn't dare mention this nagging feeling to Laney or Shelby as they would surely advise her to listen.

Fortunately, Tawna did show up right on time to pick Allie up from the airport, and Allie felt her stomach relax. Maybe she was being a worry wart for no good reason, maybe Tawna had changed. She certainly looked just as gorgeous as ever as she came towards Allie, arms outstretched blonde hair freshly highlighted and a purple sundress clinging to her admirable figure in all the right places.

"Alliiiieeeeee! I can't believe you're actually here! This is so exciting!" Tawna squealed. The two embraced and Allie noticed the strong smell of a man's cologne.

"Thank you so much Tawna for letting me crash with you. And by the smell of things it seems as though your new guy is working out quite nicely, eh?"

Tawna beamed. "Oh my god Allie, you are going to love Gerry. He is soooo amazing. I feel so lucky to have met him. I really think he might be the One."

Allie couldn't ever remember a time Tawna used the term "the One" – so who knew what could happen? And maybe Gerry was the right guy for her – stranger things had happened. She couldn't wait to meet him and see how things had changed for Tawna and if this guy might really be her "one".

Tawna chatted on and on about Gerry on their sunny and humid drive from Houston to Shorespoint. Allie was happy to listen, taking in the sites as the terrain changed from bustling, smoggy city to palm trees and the smell of the ocean. They stopped along the way for food to break up the three-hour drive. Once they arrived at Tawna's condo, Allie was ready for a nap.

"So, I was thinking..." Tawna began. "If you're up for it maybe you, me and Gerry can meet up tomorrow night for dinner and then I was thinking we could do a yoga class in the morning. What do you say?"

Allie hadn't expected Tawna to be scheduling their days since before in their email exchanges she had wanted things to be light and easy, but yoga and dinner the following night sounded good enough, so she rolled with it.

"That sounds great," she said, yawning. "After all of that time on the plane, I could use some yoga. And for now I think I need a hot shower and bed."

———

Allie awoke to the smell of coffee brewing and eggs on the stove.

"Morning sunshine! I am so excited to spend the day with you today and then have you meet my Gerry tonight. You're going to get a real taste for life on the Gulf! Oh and how do you like your eggs cooked?"

Allie barely had time to rub the sleep out of her eyes as Tawna continued to chatter on about why Gerry was so amazing and how she wanted Allie to give her an honest impression of him. Of course Allie would do her best, but she also wanted to spend time just be-ing like she and Tawna had originally agreed. Allie had never seen Tawna like this, although granted, it had been many years since they spent time together and they were grown-ups now, Allie had to remind herself.

"Oh, Tawna, you don't have to make me breakfast or take me around. I really loved our idea of doing our own thing and taking it easy over the next five days. Does that still work for you too?"

Tawna frowned, notably disappointed. "No, you're right, relaxing and going with the flow is best, I guess I'm just so excited to have someone I know and love visiting me I'm going a bit overboard."

Allie immediately felt like an asshole.

"Sweetie, I'm sorry, I don't want you to feel badly, I'm still recovering from my divorce-coma and need to take things easy, that's all."

When what Allie really should have said was, "I think I'll get my own place and we can meet up for dinner a few nights and maybe go for a walk on the beach one day." Tawna was being so sweet and generous to her, she really wanted to show her how much she appreciated the kindness. And her desire to show Allie that she had met the "one" was strong. Allie remembered when she and Marcus first met and how she couldn't wait to have him meet the people she loved the most in her world. Allie scolded herself, she needed to be more understanding of Tawna.

"Will you still go to yoga in an hour with me and dinner tonight with Gerry?" Tawna's lower lip protruded a smidge as she said this.

"Of course, that sounds great. I'll get ready now," Allie said as she rolled out of bed.

"And is scrambled okay for your eggs?"

Allie chuckled, she had no idea what had gotten into Tawna, but she felt it best to let it all go. "Sure thing sweetie, thank you."

As they walked into the The Yoga Haven studio, Allie immediately felt at ease. The energy was light and calming despite the fact that she still felt a bit jet-lagged. Buddhas, small fountains and inspiring books were placed strategically throughout the studio. Allie glanced at herself briefly in the studio mirrors, trying her best not to scowl at what she felt were huge under-eye circles from travel and flat hair from the humidity. She took a deep breath, letting herself feel the harmony of the center and trusting that all was unfolding as it was meant to – whether she looked as fresh and vital as she wanted to or not.

The instructor, Cathy, began to silence the class as Allie and Tawna set down their mats. Cathy was an older, sinewy woman with a brightness in her eyes that seemed to radiate light to all she made contact with. Her presence seemed to soothe all of those in attendance. She opened the class by reading briefly from Rumi to set the tone. The theme for the course was Love Transforms.

"Looking at my life
I see that only Love
Has been my soul's companion
From deep inside
My soul cries out:
Do not wait, surrender
For the sake of Love." - Rumi

Allie placed her hand on her heart as she felt the truth of these words enter every cell within her. Just then, Tawna leaned over and whispered, "How perfect since Gerry and I just met, right?" Allie smiled slightly. It was a perfect reminder. It was also a perfect reminder for Allie that Tawna had not once asked more than a few obligatory questions about her divorce from Marcus or where her love life was at. *Never mind that* Allie thought, *I mustn't get distracted with negative thoughts, I want to receive the fullness of this woman's wisdom through the words she shares and the asanas she leads us through.*

And so Allie imagined shooing that un-loving thought about Tawna from her mind and re-centered back into the present moment. As she did this, she felt her entire body relax as various areas experienced what she could only call surrender. By the end of the class Allie was in what well-known Law of Attraction teacher Abraham-Hicks would call her "high-flying disk." She was aligned with who-she-really-was as tears filled her eyes in gratitude while Cathy talked the participants through shivassana. In the final minutes of lying still, the whole class completely fell silent. Just then, Allie saw an image before her. It was Marcus – he had wings on his back and his hands were in the palms facing up position, his face glowing. He was giving her a gift.

The next thing she knew her eyes flew open as Cathy encouraged everyone to bring their attention and energy back into the room.

5

"Oh, you Southern men sure do have the charm!" Allie overheard Tawna giggle as she put her mat and blocks away from the class.

Sweaty, her sandy blonde hair pulled back tight and up high into a ponytail, Allie rounded the corner to find Tawna in the Yoga Haven lobby beaming brightly at a strikingly good-looking man from the yoga class. His long-blonde hair was in a low ponytail and his tan skin and effervescent blue eyes made him appear friendly and at ease. Allie awkwardly walked over to the two of them, unsure if she might be interrupting something serious or if Tawna just being her usual flirty self. It even crossed her mind that this man could be Tawna's "one" Gerry. Tawna hadn't said anything about what he looked like beyond that he was "hot".

"Allie, you've got to meet Justin. He grew up in Shorespoint and was giving me some ideas for things we can do while you're here," Tawna announced.

So…not Tawna's One. Allie adjusted her gaze from Tawna to Justin and found herself absolutely struck by not only how unbelievably handsome he was (even in an old Grateful Dead t-shirt and tan shorts) but by how their eye contact and hand shake seemed to send a dizzying spark throughout her entire body.

"Hello Justin, I'm Allie," she replied, smiling softly, feeling as though she was in a slight trance. She figured it must have been from the energetic elevation of the yoga class and feeling discombobulated over whether or not this man was Tawna's One or not.

"Allie, it's a pleasure to meet you," he replied, his Southern accent creeping in enough to make him sound even sexier than he looked. She was grateful he wasn't Tawna's "One" otherwise Tawna would surely be irritated that Allie couldn't tear her eyes from him.

Fortunately, it didn't appear that Tawna or Justin noticed the floaty, ungrounded state Allie was in. Instead, they all three stood there discussing the area along with other Gulf of Mexico sites, as well as Justin's natural love of Portland, Ore. Since his brother played football at Portland State University. Allie did what she could to participate in the conversation, smiling and nodding, adding how surprised she was by how small the world really was with only a few degrees of separation between any one individual. It was then that Justin suggested that they all head over to the Oasis natural foods café and store around the corner for green juice and lunch.

"I'm meeting a few of my friends over there and I would love to have you ladies join us, if you'd like," he said.

Tawna turned to Allie, giving her the eye to gauge her level of interest. Allie wasn't sure what was going on with her, but all she could do was nod. On one hand she would rather run back to Tawna's to give her hair and face a once-over before spending any more time in Justin's presence and on the other she was way too hungry and spacey to care. Besides, she reasoned with herself, it wasn't like lunch after yoga class with a group of people was a date or anything that she needed to be looking good for.

However, lunch turned out to be far more eventful than Allie had anticipated.

The eye locks between she and Justin continued while Justin's friend's Skye and Lucas chatted up Tawna. They regularly attempted to include Allie in the conversation, but every time Allie looked up or looked at who was speaking her eyes would automatically meet Justin's. It caught Allie off guard because somehow their eye contact seemed to contain conversations all on their own. Allie did her best to focus on the conversations happening around her, but even so, she could feel Justin's eyes on her. Whenever she perked up and added something to the conversation, she couldn't help but notice Justin watching her, a slight grin on his face.

Allie did her best not to break into her own huge grin, reminding herself of all the reasons why eye locks with a sexy stranger weren't that big of a deal. She paused when she realized "5 Reasons Eye Locks with a Sexy Stranger Don't Matter – Or Do They?!" would make the perfect title for a Cosmo article. Perhaps she should send that lead to Shelby's bestie Kathryn, who was a freelance writer. Despite her mind drifting, she quickly got back on task to review the reasons why the intense eye contact didn't matter. Number 1: Justin was far too good-looking. And let's face it really hot guys were notoriously too much work. Think Brad Pitt and Jennifer Aniston. When a man is that hot, he is bound to be more trouble than he is worth.

In fact, in high school, Allie had her own Brad Pitt – the all-around jock Paul. He was prettier than pretty, with wavy brown hair, clear, shiny olive skin and eyes that would melt any teenage girl's heart. She had been madly in love with him all through high school and after years of pining over him, she landed one extraordinary date (watching *The Princess Bride*– the Coast notoriously received films in the theater far past their city release date). But, sadly, after a late night make-out session in the parking lot at Oceanside Park, Allie's subsequent refusal to go any further than second base in his red Chevy truck, meant things were over. By Monday, he was on to another girl, Erin. She promised herself after all of that heartbreak that she would never let herself be so pathetic as to yearn for a man who was so much better looking than she was.

Number 2 reason Justin's sexy stares weren't worth

obsessing over (although making a numbered list of reasons not to like someone did border on obsessing, Allie consciously realized): he was way too young for her. She had overheard him mention something about being 25 to her 31. Everyone in the world knew that women matured faster than men. Which meant that in guy years, Justin was actually more like 18, whereas Allie was closer to 40 in maturity. Having any sort of interest in a younger man clearly meant Allie was off track. She knew maturity wise it would never be a match.

And finally, point number 3: Allie wasn't even remotely interested in long-distance love. All the missing one another, all the drama, it was too much. She was barely sure she wanted a relationship let alone one that was bound to make her lonesome. She had just re-entered the land of the living, she had to take things one step at a time. At this point, she was simply ready to maybe possibly date someone in the next 6 months – someone who lived on the Coast that is. This thought promptly depressed Allie when she realized that she pretty much knew everyone on the Coast and that none of them were datable. She shook her head slowly back and forth as if to shake off the feeling, hoping that Justin was more enthralled in Skye's conversation about gun laws in the U.S. than he was on what was racing through her mind. Allie had to bring herself back to reality. She was in Shorespoint to simply relax and be carefree, not have some meaningless travel fling or stare for hours on end into Justin's eyes.

Besides, she wasn't quite sure why she was spending so much mental energy making a case for not liking Justin. What was the harm of some long stares that seemed to be layered in meaning? She could shrug that off, couldn't she? Whatever was going on was somewhat out of her control, as her thoughts continued to pop in weighing in on the situation and almost surged in frequency as the eye contact with Justin increased.

"So, how will you be spending your time in Shorespoint Allie?" Justin's thick Southern accent interrupted her categorical calculations on why he was not a man she wanted in her life. An assessment her mind had worked through in a little less than 2 hours of knowing him.

Tawna jumped in.

"Well, I'm going to take her to the farmer's market cuz Allie just loves farmer's markets – don't you Allie? And then we're going to go to the Pier and the beach and that one little crab shack I like so much."

Allie sat stunned as she watched Tawna rattle off enough activities for two weeks, not to mention activities they had never once discussed.

"Um, well, actually the plan was that this trip was a getaway for me to relax and unwind. Tawna was incredibly generous to offer her place with the understanding that we would meet up for dinner or drinks a few times during my 5-day stay." Allie shot Tawna a stern look. What was getting into that girl?

Tawna giggled and tossed her blonde hair behind her shoulder. "Come on Allie, you didn't really think I would just leave you all alone during your time here, did you? Of course I'm gonna take care of my girl."

Allie did her best not to roll her eyes; she could feel Justin watching her and the last thing she wanted was to cause a scene. But, if he had any sort of intuition she was sure he could feel the discord happening between she and Tawna.

"Well, whatever you ladies plan on doing, I would really like to see you all again," Justin said, without taking his eyes off of Allie. "Maybe we could exchange numbers and you all could let me know when you had some time for us to go to dinner or hang out at the beach or something."

"Oh, that's a great idea Justin!" Tawna said as she whipped out her phone. "What's your number? I'll text you so you'll have mine."

Allie didn't have her phone with her, a deliberate action to take a true break from her day-to-day reality. In the airport, Allie had seen at least 3 different articles in 3 different magazines about "technology overload" and "techno vacations". She figured it couldn't hurt to take some time off from the Internet and her phone for a few days while she enjoyed the scenery and had time to reconnect with her newly improved and updated self. Only now she wished she had her phone as she watched Tawna exchange numbers with Justin. Allie had to remind herself that she was being silly. Tawna has already mentioned her "boyfriend" Gerry's name several times during the conversation, and besides, she didn't even *like* Justin.

"And, what's your number Allie?" Justin asked her point blank.

"Oh, oh I'm not using my phone a lot on this trip, I left it back at Tawna's, so just got ahead and text or call Tawna's phone and if we're not together," Allie made a point to shoot Tawna a look as she said this, "Tawna will just let me know what you all decide."

Allie sighed inside, congratulating herself. *Good girl. Now you won't have to worry about anything – like a hot and way too young guy interrupting your independent, stress-free vacation.*

―――――

"So…he was cute. And you two couldn't stop staring at each other," Tawna remarked as she drove them back to her condo.

"Yeah, he *was* cute. I don't know what was going on with all of the eye contact. It was like there was a magnet attached to both of our eyes or something. It was so weird. But anyway, a guy like that – so good-looking and young, he's lived here his whole life, he probably has all of the local girls plus several tourists wrapped around his little finger. I doubt we'll hear from him."

Allie wasn't sure why she was making so many blanket judgments about Justin, although she had a sneaking suspicion it had something to do with self-protection. She could feel the pull of their connection in her body, it was like a magnet. Somewhere within her was a very strong belief system that love equaled pain, especially after the split between her and Marcus. She knew intellectually that this wasn't true, but the thought of ever loving someone that much again and having them leave her literally sent stabbing pains of fear in her stomach. She knew that at some point in her life she was going to have to take a closer look at this pain/love story. She just wasn't sure if that time was now. But she couldn't help but remember at that exact moment the message from the yoga class and from her sister Laney – that Marcus and the break-up had actually been a gift.

Could she really allow herself to see what Marcus had done as an opportunity? Perhaps an opportunity to experience true love to an even greater depth than she had known before? She shook her head again, as if to bring herself back to reality, a reality where her husband of five years decided he didn't want to be married anymore and broke her heart. At least that was the story that seemed to resonate most with her pain/love belief system. If he could do that to her, and he knew her and he "loved" her even letting herself feel curious about Justin was a dangerous move. For now, it was better to believe that they wouldn't hear from him and that he was too hot and too young for her to even think twice about.

Tawna set the car in park as they pulled into her reserved parking space. Just then her phone started ringing. Even though Allie's head was turned the other direction, with her focus on three beautiful palm trees illuminating the entrance to Tawna's condominiums, she knew instantly who it was.

"Oh, hi *Justin*," Tawna said, emphasizing his name as she stared over at Allie. "It was so great to meet you too, Allie and I were just saying how incredibly nice you and your friends were."

"Okay, well that sounds great. Yes, I will tell her. You know Justin, Allie and I are having dinner at Olympia Grill at Pier 21 with my *boyfriend* (Tawna seemed to be adding emphasis to every third word if not for Justin's benefit then for Allie's) tonight at 7:30p. You're welcome to join us if you'd like." As she said this she caught Allie's eye mouthing "Is that okay with you?"

Allie sighed. What else could she do now – the invite was out there? She rolled her eyes and felt her stomach jump into her chest. How was she going to self-protect her way out of this? She heard Laney and Shelby reminding her to go with the

Universal flow and to allow things to unfold as they were meant to. Although, honestly, she realized that she simply could not keep up with the rate at which things were moving – Tawna's crazy talk about all of their "plans", Justin, the intense long eye contact, the invite, the phone call, now Tawna acting as matchmaker – what in the mother hell was going on Allie wondered? Even so, her head nodded yes to Tawna – seemingly on its own – and Allie, disgusted yet also feeling a slight thrill, opened the door to get out of the car.

As she walked back to Tawna's condo, a retro-70s-esque 11-story building, she could hear Tawna wrapping up the call with Justin, once again repeating, "I'll be sure to tell her" before hanging up.

"Allie!" She screamed. Allie turned around to face her, noticing that her stomach fluttered with increased intensity as she did.

"Okay, so he called and he turned down your offer to have dinner tonight?" Allie guessed. She couldn't believe how hard she was trying to push any possibility of Justin away, out loud anyway, while silently hoping for him to evaporate from her current vacation unfolding, and on the flip side also secretly wanting to see more of him.

"Nooo silly. He actually called to tell us how much he enjoyed our company and how he knows our girl time is important, *but* that he would definitely like to see *you* again before you head back to Oregon. So, it seemed natural to invite him to dinner tonight. Are you mad?"

"No, I'm not mad, I'm just, I don't know. I feel a bit nervous around him."

"You know when I met Gerry I was sick to my stomach the *entire* first week that we spent time together. Maybe you're nervous because you really like him."

"Maybe," Allie replied weakly, noting how intuitive Tawna actually was.

"Maybe he'll be your rebound from Marcus."

The thought of this made Allie's stomach fluttering turning into some gut-wrenching pains. She placed a hand on her stomach and rubbed it softly. "Am I still rebounding if it's been a year since the split? And wait — are we still doing that — rebounding? I thought we stopped rebounding after college and now we get to have grown-up relationships."

Tawna giggled. "Well, I think it's perfect. And there's nothing wrong with a rebound. They're fun! Besides, at the very least the boys will have someone to talk to while we continue to catch up."

Allie didn't want to offend Tawna and let her know they had covered just about every Tawna-topic that Allie was interested in covering for...the rest of eternity. Instead, she smiled and said, "I guess I'll have to find something cute to wear since you've got a new dress to wear tonight too."

Tawna seemed pleased with herself. "It's for Gerry. I love wearing clothes that turn him on. You should try to find something you think would turn Justin on too."

Allie frowned. She couldn't remember the last time she wore anything specifically with the intent to turn a man on.

———

Like the rising and breaking waves of the ocean that they were surrounded by, Tawna's enthusiasm for Justin and Allie's connection seemed to pass with every minute at dinner. First, Justin insisted on ordering appetizers for the table. Then, he wanted to gain a consensus from the table on the appropriate wine to choose, and finally he couldn't seem to take his eyes off of Allie. To Allie, this was all a breath of fresh air. Marcus was always so worried about money he would never be caught ordering group apps or bottles of wine for any table — including if the table was shared by him and Allie. To have a man not only take control but to be so generous stupefied Allie. Men like this existed. Men who called just to say they loved meeting you and wanted to see you again. Men who stood when you got up to go to the bathroom. Men who couldn't take their eyes off you, but also could be polite and cordial to everyone around them.

And Tawna probably wouldn't have been so annoyed had

her Gerry showed up in the same manner. But alas, he ordered the cheapest item on the menu, ran every choice and price by Tawna, suggesting they share their meal and avoided Justin's generous request for a bottle of wine for the table. In short the dinner was a bit of a fiasco for the 4 of them. Allie could feel Tawna's growing tension looking back from Justin to Gerry, squinting her eyes, as if trying to figure out how Allie could have a man who was arguably more of a gentleman and more attentive than the dude sitting next to her. It had always been Tawna's role to have a great man who lavished her with whatever she wanted. It was out of Allie and she's dynamic for the roles to be reversed. From the looks of things, Tawna was not enjoying this shift in their relationship dynamic.

Meanwhile, Allie could hardly give any real significant thought to whatever pain Tawna might have found herself in. She was simply in a state of awe over Justin. Who was this man? He made every attempt to keep the conversation flowing between the four of them, but with Tawna's angst, Allie's awe and Gerry's avoidance – he and Allie continued to exchange meaningful glances and often found themselves leaning in towards one another in their own conversation. Allie wasn't entirely sure what was going on, but she knew her relaxed, stress-free vacation had just taken a whole new turn.

———

"What should we do next?" Tawna seemed to have come out of her angst-y state in an attempt to re-direct the course of the night as everyone finished their dinner.

"Well, Allie and I could spend some time one-on-one so you two can have more time together," Justin offered.

Tawna pretended not to hear him. "Should we go to that new wine bar I just heard about in Old town or the jazz club down the road?"

"Um, why don't we start by going to the bathroom Tawna?" Allie offered. Justin stood as they got up from the table, and Allie couldn't help but smile appreciatively, touching him on the shoulder, letting her hand glide over the back of his neck. Gerry stared up at him in wonder. He was probably thinking the same thing she and Tawna were thinking – where did this guy come from? It seemed to be the question of the night, at least energetically for everyone at the table.

However, once they got to the bathroom the Tawna show re-emerged as Tawna begun gushing about how great Gerry was, pushing to get Allie's agreement.

"He seems sweet, a little quiet tonight, but maybe that's because you two need some more one-on-one time? I'm happy to get a hotel room so that we don't all try to awkwardly share your studio."

Allie could feel the knot in her stomach returning, Tawna's behavior tonight made her feel it would be better to no longer stay with her. They were two different people now and Laney had been right – staying with her after so long of not being in contact was a bad idea. And to top it off, any time Tawna and Gerry did speak up it was to say how desperate they were for more alone time, alluding to their sexual escapades. Allie had heard many of the details of Tawna's erotic exploits when they were friends back in college and Tawna had already let Allie know on more than one occasion that Gerry was quite the skilled lover. Really, Allie had to laugh about it all. She did love Tawna and her crazy stories, but honestly the last thing she wanted was to be in the same room with it.

"No! Never. I would be so offended. You'll just sleep on the couch and it will be fine."

"Tawna, the couch literally touches the Murphy bed in your studio. It will be like all three of us sleeping together."

Tawna, apparently "over" the conversation, changed the subject as she primped and played with her hair in the mirror. "So, where should we go next?" she cooed.

"I'm going to go with Justin and then I'll have him bring me back to your place late tonight, that way you and Gerry can have plenty of couple time.'"

"Oh," Tawna said as she frowned. "Are you sure?"

"Yes, of course – didn't you hear Justin say he wanted to take me out for some one-on-one time?"

"Oh." And that was all Tawna said.

But, Tawna's behavior didn't matter, because what came next made Allie so giddy she could barely think about anything other than Justin.

———

As they walked along Pier 21 admiring the beauty of the sky, Allie couldn't help but notice her whole body slightly shivering. She wasn't exactly sure why, but she knew it had more to do with the effect Justin was having on her than the outdoor temperature. Despite the oddness of Tawna and Gerry, Allie felt like she was floating through dinner on a cloud. She watched Justin intently as he watched her, and over and over she would catch her mind saying, "*Who is this guy?*" He was nothing like any man Allie had attracted before. He was confident and strong, yes, but as a man. When the bill came and Allie took out her card to pay, he simply (as he was talking with the waitress about the various events the pier held), put up his hand and said, "No, Allie, I've got this." And she could tell he meant it.

Before Marcus and even with Marcus, men would offer to pay but in a way that Allie could feel was more because they felt like they had to or should, not because they wanted to. Or sometimes they wouldn't even bother attempting to pay and would just let Allie take care of the bill. Marcus firmly believed that everything between a couple should be 50-50, and early on in their dating he had said, "Why should a guy have to pay for what his date is eating?" He didn't understand the concept of taking care of a woman in that way. At the time Allie had accepted this about Marcus; she made plenty of money and wasn't looking for someone to take care of her financially. But, she had to admit that it felt really amazing to be cared for by a man in that way. When a man took care of a woman, even in the simple way of buying her dinner, it evoked something within her that she may have trouble expressing in words. But, Allie noticed it immediately in herself. Her whole body relaxed and she felt safe and protected. She trusted a man who knew how to care for her.

Justin knew who he was and owned it fully. There was not going to be an awkward exchange, with him inevitably shrugging and saying, "Sure, we can split the bill." There was no two ways about it. He had it handled. Allie discovered that this was a huge turn-on for her. His strength and confidence drew her more to him.

Seemingly reading her thoughts (or her body), Justin reached out and placed his hand on her forearm, "I'm sorry, I'm chattering on and on about the history of this pier and didn't even see if you needed a jacket." He put his arm around her. "How about we walk over to Nonno Tony's World Kitchen," he pointed to it, across the way. "And we'll have some wine to warm you up."

Yet again, he took charge of the situation and made a decision. Allie sighed. After making virtually all of the decisions in her relationship with Marcus (other than the one to end their marriage) as to where to eat, what to do and where to go, it was incredibly refreshing to completely avoid having a back and forth conversation about who wanted to do what where, and to have the man simply make a choice for them.

"That sounds perfect." Allie replied as they walked, his arm around her, to Nonno's.

When they got to the booth they were to sit in, Justin stood and waited. Allie wasn't sure why, so she stood too. Finally, she said, "Are you waiting for something?"

He nodded and smiled, saying, "For you to sit down."

"Oh! God, I am just so not used to this kind of treatment. You Southern men really know what you're doing. Thank you so much. I've been so blown away by you all night."

"Well, it's sincere compliments like that, that inspire us to keep the chivalry going. I love it, so it's good to know you love it too." He winked as he said this, then reached for the wine list.

Who is this man? Echoed through Allie's mind yet again. Finally, she couldn't hold it in any longer.

"Who are you Justin? Like, I don't even know what to do

with this. This whole day has been like I was walking through a dream. At yoga and then at Oasis and now tonight. I feel like you're this whole other type of man that I seriously have no idea what to do with."

Justin watched her as she spoke very carefully, a small smile forming at his lips, his blue eyes dancing in the low candlelight of the restaurant. He reached out and touched her hand and said, "Maybe you're just supposed to enjoy this, enjoy me, enjoy us and then try to figure it out at a much later date."

Allie burst out laughing.

"Now, there's a novel concept. You mean, be in the moment, be here now and *then* once I'm back home analyze the hell out of it?"

Justin laughed, nodding. "Yes, I think something like that might work better or skip the whole 'analyze the hell' out of it part."

The laughter dissipated her tension. She learned that Justin was currently reading the *Bhagavad Gita*, exploring the concepts of selfless service and how he could bring more of that into his life. As a successful business owner (he ran a local CrossFit gym and a beach service business during the tourist season), Justin was at a point where he wanted his life to have greater meaning.

"Actually, before meeting you, I had given up on dating or romantic relationships. In reading the Gita, I felt like perhaps I needed to sell everything and go volunteer in India or move to somewhere more in need. That perhaps romantic love just wasn't part of the deal for me."

Allie was shocked. Justin was attractive, intelligent and easy to be around. She couldn't imagine giving up love completely, and her husband had told her he didn't want to be married anymore. Allie really hoped with all of her heart that as Laney and Shelby had hinted at and from what she saw in her yoga meditation earlier in the day – that Marcus was really giving her a gift and that love would bless her life again.

"I can't imagine giving up on love and I got divorced last year after my husband told me over breakfast that he didn't want to be married anymore.'"

Justin's face cringed in pain. He reached out, placing his hand on hers softly. "I'm so sorry Allie. That must have been devastating. How long were you married?"

"Five years. And it was pretty shocking. But today in the yoga meditation I had this image come up of Marcus, my ex, with angel wings and his hands spread out, like he was giving me a gift. My sisters are saying that's exactly what happened and I'm starting to think maybe they're on to something. I know that probably sounds crazy but maybe all of the optimists are right, maybe everything really does happen for a reason."

"That doesn't sound crazy at all, it sounds really profound. And I'm inspired hearing that even after going through something that painful that you still believe in love."

He moved his hand, but his eyes stayed locked on hers.

"Yeah, I mean I wanted to give up on love. For a year I sort of was in hiding, I am now calling it my 'divorce-coma', but even so a deeper part of me," Allie placed her hand on her heart. "Knew that this wasn't the end for me. That rather it was a new beginning and that love would find me again. And yes, I'm sure it sounds Pollyanna-ish, but I can't help it, I feel it."

She thought she saw Justin's eyes water, but he looked down and took a drink of ice water. Just then the waitress arrived ready to take their wine order. Justin again took the lead and asked to sample two of the wines that he and Allie were interested in. He was very polite and kind, but also direct. The waitress said she would be right back with their samples. Justin wiped away at his left eye, looking back up at Allie.

"You have a beautiful heart Allie. Thank you for sharing it with me. I'm sure it's not always easy to talk about these things."

"Aww...you're welcome. And thank you, Justin." Allie paused for a minute. "And you know, it feels really good to speak my truth, even on a date with a very handsome man."

Justin smiled and the waitress returned with their samples.

Not surprisingly they both loved the Louis Martini Cab and decided on it together.

The conversation continued to flow without effort and Allie still had the feeling she was walking on a cloud or floating through some kind of dream state. Justin was conscious, kind, a true gentleman in every sense of the word, spiritual, and was also successful. Not to mention gorgeous. Wait – hadn't she already noted that several times as she attempted to sum him up? He listened to her intently, asked thought-provoking questions and all of this made her feel incredibly special. In essence, he was a man, a true, empowered masculine man. He was so in his power, so rooted in his masculine that Allie was in awe. Her stomach fluttered and she caught herself wondering when the last time was that a man gave her butterflies.

She and Marcus had been so compatible that being together was easy – they liked to do all of the same things, and she didn't mind that he didn't have any money nor cared too much about taking the lead as the man in their relationship. They actually didn't experience much polarization – they were like really good friends, and they split most purchases right down the middle most of the time. Allie wasn't super in her feminine, she was just Allie, sort of plain and Marcus wasn't super masculine, he was just Marcus, sort of plain too. She always made more money than he did, but he had moved to the Coast to be with her, so she figured it all balanced out and paid for any of their extra expenses as well as created a savings account for them. Their sex life had been good, but nothing earth-shattering. Marcus always took care of her sexually, making sure she had an orgasm and then promptly followed suit. It wasn't by any means terrible, it was good, solid even. But it hadn't ever been more than a couple of times a week and it hadn't ever given her butterflies. And she was just having wine with Justin…

"Why don't we bottle this up and take it with us?" Justin cut into her thoughts. "I would love to show you the historical building I was telling you about where we built our gym. Or I can take you back to Tawna's — whatever you prefer."

"There's no way I'm going back to Tawna's — Gerry is staying the night and I'm trying to figure out what to do about that. She says she'll be 'offended' if I get a hotel room. But c'mon — staying in the studio with her and her new guy? Not exactly comfortable for me especially since she already filled me in on what an amazing lover he is. So not particularly how I want to spend the rest of my night."

Justin chuckled. "No I can imagine not. Well, just know you can always stay with me. I can sleep on the couch or something — so no funny business. But whatever you decide, don't feel stranded. You have options either way."

Allie took a deep breath and smiled. She *did* have options. And right now the option of staying with Justin trumped anything else that she had going on.

6

A cockroach scurried across the floor of the gym and Allie screamed. Immediately Justin was by her side. "What happened?" he asked.

"Oh. My. God." Allie said as she stared and pointed in the direction of the cockroach. "A gigantic cockroach just scurried across the floor."

Justin burst out laughing, grabbing his side with one hand, his other hand on Allie's shoulder. "You screamed…over…a cockroach?" He said in between breaths.

His laughter was contagious and Allie also began to laugh. "Well, yeah, they're…disgusting."

Justin stood straight up, placing his arm fully around Allie. "Listen Allie, when you're with me you don't have to worry about cockroaches. I will totally protect you." His voice was serious now and he looked her square in the eye. The laughter stopped. Their faces were close together and Allie didn't dare breathe.

"Okay, thanks," she whispered.

He took her hand and led her through the building into an area where he and his business partner had begun to collect reclaimed wood for their next business venture. Allie was impressed, Justin was certainly motivated; he was definitely a man who went after what he wanted. His spiritual exploration combined with his drive to have an impact on the world inspired Allie. *Men like this actually exist.* As far as she could tell, Justin was the total package – fully in his masculine while also connected and open spiritually. Laney and Shelby would be so proud of her for attracting a man like this into her life (and she hadn't even done anything to summon him other than follow the signs to visit and she had to hand it to Tawna, follow her inspiration to the yoga studio!). She almost felt like texting her sisters' right then, but when Justin grabbed her hand to lead her out of the building, she decided against it.

"So…that's the grand tour," he announced.

"It's really awesome what you're creating Justin," Allie said, meaning every word of it.

"Well, I'm not sure about awesome, but I can't seem to stop. It's important to me to have as much of an impact as I can for healthy living. Still…you know, I wonder if my time would be better spent volunteering in a country where people really need the support. But for now, I'm supporting my local community…" His voice trailed off.

"What is it?" Allie asked.

"It's just…well, for some reason I can't stop thinking about our conversation back at the restaurant." Justin took her hand and led her to a small bench outside of the building. "You know when you were saying that even after your husband did that stupid thing and ended the marriage. Is it okay to say that? Because I think that guy is a total idiot. A woman like you is not something to mess with. If a man is fortunate enough to be with someone like you, he better hang on for dear life." Justin's eyes met hers and she could feel a soft heat cover her body, from her pelvis to her crown.

"It is 100 percent okay for you to say that. And thank you. It's extremely kind of you, especially since you've only known me for like what – 5 minutes?" She chuckled and Justin smiled.

"It's true we haven't known each other long, but I consider myself an excellent judge of character. I have not been on a date or spent time with a woman in three years. And you know why? Because in that three years I have not met a woman who inspired me to want to be anything other than alone. And there are some great women in the world, but you, the second I saw you I felt something in my body I've never felt before. I felt my heart pull, like my chest was expanding and opening towards you. I knew right then that you were worth being with."

Justin's hand was now resting on Allie's thigh and Allie could feel her heart pounding so loudly that she could barely access her own thoughts. Three years? And suddenly it was her. She hadn't even done anything. She hadn't even really smiled at him or spoken up. How could he have felt anything? As if reading her mind, Justin continued.

"And no, you didn't do anything to activate our connection. But it was there. I felt it, and I have never felt anything like that before."

Allie sat quietly as her mind attempted to understand what he was saying. She felt flushed and cold and hot all at the same time. It was like her body was trying to communicate with her what this all meant and why it was happening, but her mind could not get a hold of it. Justin leaned in, bringing Allie's eyes back to his.

"Too much? Am I freaking you out?"

"No," Allie shook her head. "No you are absolutely *not* freaking me out. My mind is trying to understand what is happening right now and it's not really able to. The fact that I'm even here in Shorespoint is totally on a whim. Tawna and I haven't spoken or seen each other in years. I couldn't even really tell you why I came here, the opportunity presented itself and now, here I am. In front of you, and I'm completely in awe of you. I have never met a man like you. It's, it's, it's leaving me a bit speechless actually."

Justin nodded while Allie spoke, squeezed her leg and then removed his hand.

"It's wild, right? We think we are headed one direction and then the Universe/God – whatever you want to call it – comes in and redirects us completely. I wanted to have a good yoga class. I needed to stretch my body. This is one of the busiest times in my business – I should be working not falling for—" Justin stopped himself, smiling embarrassingly like he had shared too much, quickly though he regained his composure. "I should be living the life I had been living for the past three years – quite happily I might add – but instead, I'm here with you and it's the only place I want to be."

Justin leaned in and Allie braced herself – her first kiss in over a year. What would it be like? How would it feel? Unfortunately, she still wouldn't know because Justin leaned in for a hug. Allie sighed. Relieved and disappointed all at once. The perfect man who doesn't make a move? Boy would Laney and Shelby enjoy this story...

––––––

"So, do you want to come up?" Justin stood at the foot of the stairs in the historic building where his CrossFit gym and reclaimed wood business resided. As it turned out, he also lived in the upstairs space.

"Are there cockroaches?" Allie hedged.

Justin laughed. "I told you, when you're with me, they will not bother you. I promise."

"Okay, so you're saying there are cockroaches but you'll kill them for me?"

Justin rolled his eyes and grabbed Allie's hand. "You're coming with me."

––––––

Upon entering Justin's loft apartment, she suddenly realized what his flaw was – he did not clean his house ever or believe in organization of any kind. Pizza boxes, green juice bottles, clothes, towels and half eaten plates of food littered Justin's apartment. Allie's eyes scanned the room in horror. *This is what three years without a woman in your life will do,* she silently thought to herself. She noticed her mouth was slightly open in utter disbelief, she quickly closed it hoping Justin didn't see the full level of judgment she was feeling for his abhorrent housekeeping skills.

"Um, okay, so, this one is hard to explain," he said as he scratched the back of his head. "Did I mention I haven't had a woman in my life in three years?" He scrunched his face as he looked at her. "Are you completely mortified?"

"Well, completely is probably too strong of an adverb for the level of mortification I'm feeling," Allie teased. Or sort-of-kind-of teased.

"I know, even my dad gives me a hard time about this. I'm just so busy I don't have time to clean-up. And, obviously, I had no idea I would be bringing you here tonight or I would have done something about it." Justin began walking through the space, picking things up and dusting off the couch which was covered in clothes. "Here, take a seat and I'll make some space for us."

Allie gingerly walked over to the couch, inspecting it for bugs or anything else that might be on or in it.

"And don't worry – there are no cockroaches Allie. I promise."

She looked up at him not entirely convinced and nodded. She sat down and uncomfortably looked around her. Justin caught her eye and smiled. She had no choice, she had to smile back. His face was too gorgeous and his eyes too kind not to. Then, they both burst into laughter.

———

"...After a couple of years it became apparent that we wanted different things. She became obsessed with how she looked, wanted the biggest house in the neighborhood, a nicer car than her friends – not that there's anything wrong with those things, but she wanted them in competition with other people around her. It was all coming from a mind place, not from her Soul wanting that expansion. And to top it off, all of her friends started having babies, so again, competition came up and suddenly she wanted to have babies – like ASAP. I loved our abundant lifestyle, but I didn't want to have to upgrade every time the neighbors did. That's not how I want to live, I want to live from my Soul and let that be my guide. When I put my foot down about all of that, we unfortunately just continued to grow further apart. Soon, we became unrecognizable to one another. And she essentially became someone I wouldn't even be friends with."

Allie nodded her head as she listened to Justin share his story about why he had given up on love. They were sitting on his now fully cleaned off brown leather love seat with their feet propped up on his fully clear brown-black IKEA coffee table, angling their bodies towards one another, a glass of red wine in hand.

"So yeah, there was that," he laughed, smiling a bit nervously.

"Wow, I can't imagine how that must have felt. You know they say people grow apart – it happens all the time, but to be in it when it's happening is really tough."

"I believe we as human beings are constantly evolving and I embrace that fact. However, I imagine that it would be pretty amazing to evolve with someone, to both expand together. I thought that would happen for Angela and I, but it didn't. And since I thought she was the woman I was going to marry and spend my life with, when it fell a part I shut that part of myself that could love deeply down. I haven't even thought about the kind of relationship I would want until right now, in this moment with you. It's like I totally gave up on love – I wouldn't even let myself think about it. Hearing your story of how you didn't give up on love even after your husband said he didn't want to be married anymore really inspired me. It gives me a lot to think about."

"I wouldn't say I didn't give up – a part of me was crushed when he left and I took the past year to be with myself. And when I say be with myself, I mean that I virtually didn't see anyone beyond who I had to see at work and for the holidays. I even dodged my sisters a lot, and I love them! It was a really intense time, but primarily because that's the space I put myself in and that's the space I wanted to be in on many levels. Sort of like marinating in the suffering. I can see now I didn't have to choose that path, but I did and for whatever reason it was what I needed to do. Even so, looking back I can see that some part of me knew that I would eventually love again. There was no way that I could admit defeat around love forever, you know? It's the most important thing in the world. It doesn't matter how many times you've loved and lost love – it's still the most vibrant energy that keeps the human race going – at least I think so anyway. How have the past three years been, did you miss having a woman in your life?"

Justin paused and reflected on this for a bit.

"Hmm…good question. Well, I keep myself really busy, with my business, my friends and my family. I think the thoughts may have popped in about missing having a woman in my life, but if they did I immediately pushed them out. You know, men are good at compartmentalizing like that. I honestly felt really happy with my life, that I could continue on forever and be fine."

Allie was surprised. Even in her darkest moments in grieving the loss of her marriage to Marcus, she had felt a sliver of hope, of inspiration of something deep within saying, *you will love again.* She felt complete sure, but also knew that life had a richness that could not be duplicated as a single person when one was deeply in love. At the same time she also knew that being alone was far better than being in relationship with someone who was not the right match, let alone someone who thought breakfast was the perfect time to end a 5-year marriage. Maybe she was closer to seeing the break-up as a gift after all…

Justin continued. "But now, in meeting and connecting with you Allie, I feel like the Universe/God is reminding me of the importance of having someone special that you care deeply about in life. It's like I forgot, then I saw you at Yoga Haven and everything shifted for me."

Allie stared into his beaming blue eyes. She felt the solidarity in the words he spoke, she felt his conviction and passion and the power of his focus. She found all of this to be beyond sexy, it was like who-he-was as a man and as a human being made her want to love again, made her want to get to the other side of her healing process and dive deeply into love, into the passion of a man who was a man in the fullest sense. A man who could love a woman eternally while not losing his own need to create and impact the world.

All of this made Allie sigh.

"Justin…I…"

"Listen, I know it's a lot to take in, so don't feel like you have to say anything back to me. I just want you to know exactly how I feel. I know we have limited time – you have your friend and only three more days here, so I want you to know what an impact meeting you is having on me. That's it. So…let's change the subject, shall we? How about we go check out that moon?" With that, Justin got up from the couch, grabbed Allie's glass of wine and then put out his hand to pull her up.

Allie smiled. This guy was good, there was no question about it.

7

Allie opened the door quietly, tip-toeing into Tawna's studio. She saw Tawna and Gerry entwined on the Murphy bed, sound asleep. She smiled. Even with all of Tawna's quirks, she loved that she had found love and was enjoying her life. That's all that really mattered anyway, she thought. Love and enjoying this life. When you boil it all down, if you can do those two things, you'll die feeling good about the life you lived. Allie quickly sent Justin a text – she promised him she would once she got back up to Tawna's studio. The time said 5:30am and Allie could not believe it. She hadn't stayed up all night with a man since she was 19.

The walk with Justin on the beach had been the perfect way to end their date. They strolled hand in hand often in silence taking in the beauty of nature all around them. At one point they stopped and stared at the moon, brilliantly lighting up the sky as the sun began to creep its way up, faintly coloring the sky. Justin stood behind her, his arms wrapped around her, his chin nestled in the crook of her neck and shoulder. They stood like that for what seemed like hours, admiring the beauty of the earth, feeling gratitude for being together in that spectacular moment with one another.

Allie had whispered at one point, "I will remember this for

the rest of my life."

Justin squeezed her tight, "As will I Allie, as will I," he said as he kissed her head softly.

It was all so utterly perfect right then. Their connection was undeniable, their former heartbreaks had opened the door for deeper and greater love to come in, their desire to expand was strong – it was all so aligned that Allie couldn't bear to think about what would come next. She was absolutely and totally in the moment with Justin. It was too precious and too sweet to do anything else; fast-forwarding to the future would have only diminished the high quality of the vibration that they were sharing together. And there was no way in hell she was about to do that.

As the sky filled with an orange hue, they walked hand-in-hand back to where his white Ford F150 truck was parked. (It was not lost on Allie that this seeming knight of a man also came in on a white horse of sorts. She wanted to high-five the Universe for its cute joke.) As they got to his truck, Justin went to the door to open it for her and then stood directly in front of her. He wrapped his arms around her and squeezed her tight. She buried her face in his chest and said, "I don't want it to end. I know I need to go back, but I don't want to."

He whispered in her ear, "I know, I feel the same. But hey, you've got three days, let's spend as much time together as we can."

He pulled her back, looking at her, "If you want to, I know you have time to spend with Tawna too."

Allie rolled her eyes. "Coming down here was never about Tawna. Sure, we were going to catch up and we truly have over the past two days. The rest of the time was always meant for me to relax and reset after the year of healing I've had. And I honestly could not think of a better way to reset than to spend this time with you Justin."

He brushed back a piece of her hair, tucking it carefully behind her ear and smiled. "Looks like I needed a reset too. So, thank you. And since that's the case for both of us, I want to spend the next three days with you. Deal?"

Allie giggled. Was this really happening?

"Deal."

Then, instead of going back for another hug, Justin guided his hand along Allie's face, cupping it at her jaw and slowly leaned in. His breath was hot, his hand warm and comforting on her face. Allie felt her chest rise and fall as her heart picked up speed. This *was* really happening.

His lips touched hers and she felt a pulsing in her yoni. Their bodies came fully together instinctively and it was as though Allie could feel their chakras somehow aligning in that one moment. She opened her mouth slightly and felt the gentleness of his kiss. He was taking his time, very carefully and lightly allowing his lips to meet hers. Allie felt her eagerness rise, wanting to grab him harder and lose herself in his kiss. But she waited; she wanted to experience what he was leading her to. She wanted to know what kissing a man like this could really be like. His tongue softly glided into her mouth, causing her to give out a slight moan. It was so gentle, so intentional that she felt her whole body opening to him.

He wrapped his arms around her body nuzzling his face into her hair, breathing in deeply as if taking her all in.

"Wow." Was all Allie could say,

"Wow is right," Justin murmured back.

He pulled back. "I don't know why it took me so long to do that, but I couldn't let you leave without a kiss. I just couldn't."

"Nor should you of. Thank you." This time it was Allie who leaned in, wrapping her arms tightly around his neck, allowing her tongue to enter his mouth and feel the warmth and heat within him. Justin responded strongly, moving her back up against the truck, pressing his body into hers, allowing their mutual passion for one another to be felt in every cell of their bodies. Allie wanted more. She wasn't sure she was ever going to make it back to Tawna's with this turn of events.

After about 10 minutes of passionate kissing pressed up against Justin's white horse Ford, they retreated into the quiet knowing that it was time to part.

———

And now she was back at Tawna's feeling the intense command of her intuition telling her to get out, get a hotel and spend the next three days with Justin and Justin only. But, Allie's mind attempted to reason – Tawna said she would be offended and the last thing she wanted was to hurt her feelings or have any drama. Maybe there could be a way that she could do it all…

As Allie crawled onto the couch listening to the snoring of Tawna and Gerry, she couldn't help but smile. For the first time she felt the full truth of what her sisters Laney and Shelby had always told her – everything really was working out *for* her.

———

A few hours later she heard Tawna and Gerry up, preparing breakfast as Gerry got ready to head off to work in Houston.

"Baby, do you want cream in your coffee?" Gerry called to Tawna.

"Yes, please baby, that would be perfect," Tawna cooed back.

Tawna must have heard Allie stirring because she peaked over the couch and met Allie's eyes. "Well, well, well look who's here. What time did you get in missy?" Tawna playfully scolded.

Allie laughed. "You do not want to know. But I will tell you it was the best date of my life. So thank you Tawna for letting me crash at your place and visit Shorespoint. Justin is quite possibly the most amazing man I've ever met."

Gerry must have been eavesdropping because he came right over with Tawna's coffee. "Really Allie? That is so awesome! Are you guys going to see each other again?"

Tawna's face dropped, as though the possibility of this being more than a one-nighter had not yet crossed her mind. Allie stalled. Of course she was going to see him again; she had just had the best date of her life. But she could tell that Tawna, for whatever reason, did not like the sound of this.

"Well Allie, are you going to see him again?" Tawna pressed.

"Yes, of course. I have three days left and we want to spend as much time together as we can. Since you and I didn't have any set plans and had said we would both do our own thing and meet up occasionally, I figured that would be okay."

Tawna sipped her coffee and nodded. Gerry must have felt the tension in the room because he suddenly had to get going to work, right away.

"Okay ladies, I've got to go. Baby – I'll talk to you tonight and see you tomorrow?" Gerry seemed to be asking a question so Allie piped in.

"Tawna, just like I told you before I came down – spend all the time you two want together and maybe the four of us can have dinner again or something."

Tawna walked over to Gerry and kissed him. "Yes, baby call me later and we can work out the rest of the details."

Allie rolled her eyes to herself. Why did Tawna suddenly care about what she was doing? Pre-Justin on the scene, Tawna had mentioned several times that Gerry would be around for a lot of the week. But now she was acting like plans had somehow changed.

Once Gerry left Tawna came back into the room, her eyes bright.

"So...tell me everything about Justin. I want to hear all about the best date of your life!" Tawna seemed to have composed herself and was back in cheery-it's-all-good mode.

"God, there's so much. Just everything he did was so amazing..."

Tawna interrupted. "Oh, I know, that's totally how I feel about Gerry. Just so amazing. What did you think of him? Can you see us together?"

Allie laughed inside. She had barely gotten anything out and here they were again – talking about Tawna. Not that she totally minded. People change and grow and she couldn't expect that Tawna would somehow grow into a person who genuinely wanted to talk about anything other than herself.

"I like Gerry, he seems totally sweet and really adores you. I love that!"

"I know, right? But can you see us being together long-term, like forever?"

Allie wasn't sure how to answer this.

"I didn't think forever was something you were interested in Tawna."

"Well, you know, we're getting older – it's definitely something I think about from time to time. Gerry drops the "forever" word every now and again and I'm just not totally sure. You know last night at dinner watching Justin with you made me wish Gerry could be more in his masculine like that. Take charge, make decisions. And having a man who can pay for things and isn't always broke…well, that would be a dream."

Allie had to agree. Those aspects of Justin really appealed to her too. She loved being in his presence – a man who fully embodied his masculine energy and was also connected spiritually made her feel more alive than she had ever experienced with other men. But she didn't want to dog Gerry, he was a good guy. She honestly couldn't see Tawna with him forever, but it was hardly her place to dish out that opinion.

"Yeah, there are always areas that a man or anyone can grow in. But Gerry seems to really love you and isn't that what matters most?"

Tawna sighed, twirling her hair. "I suppose," she said. "It's just that seeing you with Justin really brought up a lot for me. Like maybe I need to keep dating so I can find someone like that rather than wasting time hoping Gerry will step more into his masculine…"

Allie put her hand on Tawna's. "Sweetie, do whatever you feel is right for you, but comparing is never a good idea. I'm just getting to know Justin – and surely he has areas he needs to grow in as well. I'm sure when you first met Gerry you didn't know all of this, right?"

"So you really are going to spend more time with him?"

"Of course, why wouldn't I?"

Tawna bit her lip, feigning a pout. "I just thought we were going to spend more time together."

Allie sighed. "Tawna, we haven't seen each other in years and I've had a great time with you. I'm totally down with spending today together but I would really like to spend the evening with Justin to see where this thing might go. It feels important to me. I haven't had a connection with someone like this in a long time."

Tawna did not seem the slightest bit impressed. Instead she got more irritated. "It's not like vacation hook-ups ever last anyway Allie. You probably won't see this guy ever again."

Well that was not super helpful, Allie thought to herself. She didn't want to have to spend time with Tawna out of obligation or to avoid discord between them. Allie began to feel anger boiling under the surface within her. Who did Tawna think she was? Did she really expect that Allie would want to spend all of her time talking about her and doing solely what she wanted to do? Allie bit her lip, remembering Laney's cautioning her to get a hotel room because it had been such a long time since she and Tawna had been together. Allie reflected on that heavy feeling in her stomach on the days leading up to the trip. Some part of her had known that details of the trip were not in alignment. She should have paid more attention to Laney and to that heavy feeling in her body. But what the hell Tawna? Why did she even care? Finally, Allie could not hold back her frustration any longer.

"Well thank you for your support Tawna, I totally appreciate your positivity. It's completely unfair for you to suddenly decide you want to dominate my time when that was never the plan nor what I wanted."

"Your girlfriends should be more important to you Allie," Tawna obviously was going to pull out all the stops on this one in order to get her way.

Allie had to laugh. When she and Tawna had known one another in college, Tawna was frequently known for skipping out early on girl's nights or being unavailable for weeks or months at a time depending on who she was in a relationship with. Allie, on the other hand, never had this problem. She always had weekly dates with her girlfriends and found a comfortable balance in being with her man and her girls when she and Marcus were married, and before then.

"Tawna, I'm pretty sure you're projecting right now. I have no problem making time for my friends. This is a unique situation and I am asking that you be understanding and supportive. It's an awesome turn of events and I feel so grateful to have met Justin. Can't you be happy for me instead of ruminating on your expectations?"

Now it was Tawna's turn to roll her eyes. "Whatever. You guys should go on a date tomorrow night or something. But tonight I want to have a girl's night with you. I already told Gerry about it and invited a couple of my other girls."

Oy vey. Allie was not having much success. She didn't want to have drama with Tawna but she also didn't want to spend any more time with her either. She found her behavior totally manipulative and unsupportive. Something about Tawna seeing Justin with Allie had triggered her and now she was going all out to squash their time together in whatever way she could. Allie knew the only reason Tawna was pushing for a girl's night (which hadn't all of their time been that other than dinner with Gerry & Justin – and that was totally Tawna's idea?) was because Gerry was working. But whatever. Allie could suck it up for one more night – after that she would spend her remaining two nights with Justin.

"Okay, Tawna, fine. I will go out with you and your girls tonight and then I'm seeing Justin Sunday night. I can't believe this is such a problem for you." Allie got up shaking her head, as her inner guidance screamed "get out of there!" She brushed the notion aside certain it would only cause more drama with Tawna – the one thing she was desperately trying to avoid.

If only Allie had listened to her intuition.

———

Girls night as Tawna had titled it consisted of eating bad food at the Crystal Cantina – which turned out to be a biker bar –

just the two of them, followed by drinks at Art Space a bar which was where a lot of disenchanted hipsters hung out to complain about what was wrong with – well, everything – followed by karaoke at Touché, a local tequila bar.

And right before leaving for their "girls" night Allie noticed that her head was pounding. She didn't usually get headaches so this was a surprise to her. She tried massaging her neck and trapezes muscles, and when she did, she noticed that they were incredibly knotted up. She remembered the energy tapping tool that Shelby & Laney had given her recently called Cortices from the healing modality BodyTalk, a modality that Shelby and Daniel used regularly. Shelby was even receiving twice-monthly sessions to support a smooth pregnancy and to help with delivery.

She quickly tapped it out before they left; taking deep breaths like Laney had instructed using her focus and her hands to balance the left and right hemispheres of her brain. Laney had insisted it was excellent for pain management and balancing the body-mind-Spirit, while Shelby had instructed her to use it as a way to "connect back to Source." Either way, Allie figured she could use all of the above for a night that looked to be going from bad to worse.

Tawna had invited several girls out to join them but only her friend Stacy was able to make it. Fortunately for Allie, Stacy was a bubbly, lovely and soothing presence amidst the awkward tension between her and Tawna. As Allie inquired about Stacy's job and what brought her to Shorespoint, she watched as Tawna proceeded to get very, very drunk. Allie decided she had better stop drinking since she knew someone was going to have to get them home and it certainly was not going to be Tawna. Tawna kept trying to get Stacy and Allie to drink more, but Stacy had things to do the next day and also needed to get home soon. She wasn't interested in a "crazy" girl's night, just drinks and food with some ladies. Allie was grateful for Stacy's presence. Ever since the talk she had with Tawna earlier that day she had a hard time even making eye contact with her let alone conversation.

Allie's felt like what must be at the heart of Tawna's desire to get her and Stacy drunk was rooted in her desire to control the situation and make Allie unavailable for Justin – a man Tawna obviously considered a catch – something she felt she deserved but not Allie. This completely baffled Allie. It wasn't an either or Universe. There was enough love and adoration for everyone in the world. And Allie knew that each person was uniquely drawn to love the person they loved because the relationship and that person had important lessons for them. It wasn't a matter of there being a finite amount of men or women or love relationships. Allie didn't understand why Tawna was behaving like she was in high school. But whatever the story going on for her, Allie wanted to get as far away as possible.

Touché was packed with "kids" in their twenties who were, like Tawna, intent on getting wildly ripped on tequila. The karaoke blared as an obviously tipsy girl belted out Tina Turner's *What's Love Got to Do With It* in what could only be described as blood curdling screams. Allie rubbed her temples; she really needed and wanted to get out of there.

With that, she stood up, without even thinking, and began to walk away.

"Where are you going Allie?" Tawna shouted out at Allie.

"Oh, just to the bathroom," Allie waved her hand, never turning back to face Tawna directly. She sighed as she felt her temples tighten and her headache intensify. Her chest seemed to be pounding with every beat to the tune of "get away from this girl and go to a hotel."

Once in the stall, Allie began furiously tapping Cortices again. What was going on with her body? The last thing she needed was to get sick in the middle of a situation she felt trapped in. She didn't want more drama, but she couldn't stand being around Tawna. She hadn't heard from Justin since earlier that day and felt like all of the negative energy between she and Tawna was somehow interfering with their ability to connect. As she was tapping out her limbic or emotional brain by holding both sides of her head and then tapping over her head and heart, Allie received a flash of inspiration. She needed to talk to Laney & Shelby, they would know the best way for her to handle the sticky situation she had gotten herself into.

Girls I need ur help. Tawna is being really controlling and I met a g8 guy! Not sure how to handle and now my body is doing weird things. Ideas? Xo

She began tapping Cortices again, taking deeper breaths as she felt her heart finally begin to slow down, knowing that help from her sisters was on the way. She expected another text back but instead, her phone began ringing. She grabbed it immediately, stopping mid-Cortices only to hear Justin's voice on the other end of the line.

"Hey beautiful! How's your girls' night?"

Allie laughed. Partly out of nervousness (she wasn't accustomed to men calling her beautiful as though it were her name) and partly because her girls night was a farce. It should have been called Tawna's attempt at control. She wasn't sure how much of the girl drama she wanted to tell Justin. It was rather embarrassing that her girlfriend was trying to actively squash her vacation awesomeness.

"Hey you! It's going...it's going good I guess. Tawna is getting wasted on tequila shots but her friend Stacy is really sweet, so that's a bonus."

"Oh, so what Tawna really meant was that she wanted a DD for the night and that's why you two had to spend tonight together?"

She loved that Justin could also see through what was happening.

"Yeah, something like that. How's the engagement party?"

Justin had shared with Allie that girl's night was just fine because he had a previous commitment to attend the engagement party of a close childhood friend. He hadn't been super thrilled to attend since he hadn't seen his friend for quite some time, but felt the fact that Allie was obligated elsewhere was an indication that they both needed to attend to their commitments.

"It was well, you know, the usual. There was a keg,

expensive gifts and everyone talking about how they knew that Jared & Samantha would be together forever from the very start. A little bit nauseating, paired with good food and beer."

Allie was surprised by his cynicism. "So...you're not a fan of folks who know when they've met the person they are going to be with forever?" She said cautiously. She didn't want to open up a huge discussion while she sat in a bathroom stall, but she also wanted to understand more about his point of view.

"Ah, hmm...I don't know actually. It just seems so trite. I certainly didn't think Jared & Samantha would last past the summer that they met, Jared had never been into one woman forever so to hear everyone say they saw it all along seems a bit ridiculous to me. And sure, I would love to believe in being with one person for the rest of your life, but I have yet to see it really work."

"What about your parents, aren't they still together?"

Justin cleared his throat, maybe she was pushing him too far. "They are, but it's not the kind of relationship I would like to have. But Allie I have to ask, where are you right now? There's a crazy echo whenever you talk."

Allie was so busted.

"I'm in a bathroom stall tapping this energy technique my sisters gave me called Cortices. I have a splitting headache and I'm trying to get rid of it. So maybe not the best location for this conversation..."

Justin laughed. "That is so awesome. Tell me you're not sitting on the toilet going to the bathroom at the same time as this conversation is taking place..."

"I'm not!" Allie shouted out. Just then she heard the familiar click of heels followed by Tawna's voice, "Allie, what are you doing in there? Why is it taking you so long?"

Justin must have heard her because he responded immediately with, "What is she, your mother now?"

"I know," Allie said, lowering her voice into the phone. "Can we meet up later?"

"For sure, I'll be done in about an hour, so call me, okay?"

he said.

"Yes, I will. Have fun at the party!"

"And hey Allie?" Justin said.

"Yes?"

"That headache is your body's way of trying to tell you something, so you may want to ask it what the message is."

Allie shook her head and smiled. Not only had she not considered this fact but she knew her sisters would be so proud of her for attracting a man who did.

———

"Were you just talking to Justin on the phone?" Tawna asked snottily.

"Uh, yes Tawna I was," Allie said as she washed her hands.

"Why are you doing this?" Tawna squealed as she raised her voice an octave higher.

Allie looked at her incredulously. "Why am I doing what Tawna?"

"Why are you choosing him over me?"

Allie sighed. Here she was a full resident in crazy town, population of two.

"You think that because I am having a wonderful, soulful connection with a man that I met while crashing at your place and who I now want to spend time with, that I am making a choice of him over you. Really Tawna? What are we working with here, a sixth grade mentality?

Tawna rolled her eyes. "That's right Allie, you're the mature one and I'm stupid. You always choose other people over me."

Allie was shocked. That's what this was really about. Something that had happened years ago that Tawna was holding on to. A story she was keeping going by her attention and belief that when it came to her and Allie, Allie would choose someone else. Allie had no idea where this stemmed from. Sure they had been close friends in college, but that was ages ago and even then being close friends wasn't about much more than Allie being her sidekick and enjoying all of her great stories and conquests. But it was true that as time went on

Allie and Tawna didn't have anything in common. Early on in college it was easy to bond over books and boys and drinking, but as they both grew, Allie did choose to spend more of her time with others she felt a deeper connection to. She had always considered that part of evolving and growing up – some people from high school and college you would stay close to and others you would not. It had never occurred to her that Tawna might have been storing that as a personal story of abandonment by Allie. Allie could see how if Tawna had processed their growing apart/up in a way that was negative to her, that it would be hurtful and that it had locked them both into an old dynamic that was no longer serving either one of them – clearly.

Even so, Allie had to hand it to Tawna. This somewhat crazy situation was helping Allie tune in to more than the actual events that were transpiring. Besides Allie realized in this moment that she had been doing the exact same thing as Tawna – keeping the story running of Tawna as the self-absorbed, controlling, manipulative girl she had felt she was years ago. And maybe she never was any of that. Allie softened as she could see Tawna's little girl desiring attention and love not some psycho friend who needed to dominate every interaction or who was jealous of the man she had attracted.

"Tawna, I'm so sorry you feel that way. I have never felt like I've chosen anyone over you, but I completely understand that has been your experience. I've been having my own experience of you as well and it seems clear that we are both operating on false pretenses. Why don't we talk about this in the morning when we are both more clear-headed?"

Even in Tawna's drunken state, she seemed to resonate with what Allie was saying and Allie could see her softening a little inside as well. Unfortunately, the alcohol was so strong in her, Tawna's soul wasn't able to catch up to let Tawna's personality know what had happened.

"Well, you do! You always ditch me for people you like better and I am just sick of it! I can't take it Allie and I won't take it! I want you out of my house immediately!"

With that Tawna slammed the bathroom door and Allie could hear as her platform heels pounded the tile back out to the bar.

Allie had just been broken up with, by an old friend she wasn't even really friends with anymore, in a tequila bar bathroom. Her night had just gotten awesome. She couldn't help but smile. The Universe was working in some really mysterious ways during her "laid-back" vacation.

———

When Allie got back to the bar, Tawna was gone, but Stacy was still sitting at their table, a slight frown on her face.

"Where did Tawna go Stacy?" Allie inquired with a slight sigh.

Stacy shrugged. "I don't really know. She stormed out of the bathroom, grabbed her things and said, 'She chose him over me!' and booked it out of here. She grabbed that guy she had been flirting with, so I'm hoping he is taking her home or she'll have the sense to get a cab. She didn't even give me time to respond."

"Oh, I'm sorry. What drama! She told me I couldn't stay with her anymore. So annoying. My intuition had been telling me to leave and get a hotel room practically since I arrived. And now all of my stuff is at her place, I have no key to get in and she is furious with me. Ugh." Allie rubbed her temples as she sat back down at the table.

Stacy rubbed her back lightly. "Well, since you chose him over her," She stopped to giggle. "Then maybe you should just go be with him."

Allie turned her head to look at her. "But I didn't choose anyone over anyone. I am just having this awesome connection with this man in the middle of my mini-getaway and Tawna is turning it into being all about her and about everything that was ever wrong with her and I's friendship."

Stacy nodded. "There are always two sides and perspectives to every relationship. Tawna was having and has been having her experience and you are having yours. No one is wrong and no one is right. It just is. Let her throw a fit, she is a big girl and needs to be responsible for her own emotions, that isn't your job. And in the meantime, you might want to take some time to get clear on what this guy means to you. It sounds like it might be pretty significant."

And that's the thing about life, you just never know when the Universe is going to deliver wisdom from some seemingly random stranger. Allie shook her head in disbelief. Not only was Stacy 100 percent right about all of it, Allie had been giving entirely too much energy to Tawna and not enough to the fact that Justin had entered her life.

She leaned over and gave Stacy a big hug. "Thank you so much Stacy, you have no idea how much everything you said impacted me. You are incredible!"

Stacy gave her a squeeze back and then picked up her purse and headed out the door. Allie ordered a glass of wine and settled in. She had some clarity she needed to connect with and a headache to release.

8

Justin's large white Ford rolled down The Block and right in front of Allie. She felt her heart pick up its pace and butterflies flutter throughout her stomach. She had sent him a text with minimal information asking him to pick her up. There was a conversation they needed to have. Allie felt lighter and she was pretty sure it wasn't just from the wine.

"Well, well, well look who's here standing on The Block waiting for me," Justin said as he got out of his truck to get Allie's door. She smiled, still amazed by a man who went so totally out of his way for her. Chivalry was not only not dead; it was blossoming in every moment!

"Yeah, you know, I was walking around down here all by my lonesome and heard the big roar of your large engine and just knew I had to wait for you to pick me up," Allie said as she winked. Justin grabbed her hand to help her into the truck and leaned in to kiss her.

As Justin got back in the truck he said, "So, I take it that girl's night is over?"

"Um, that is sort of the understatement of the year, actually." Allie replied.

He smiled and reached over to squeeze her hand. "Well, I for one am very happy to hear about this turn of events. Now, why don't we go over to Club 11 and you can tell me all about it." The thought of going to a club did not appeal to Allie but something within her said "yes" so she nodded in agreement.

When they arrived at Club 11, she was thrilled to see that it was a jazz club – not a nightclub – and was filled with incredible jazz beats and skilled musicians. The whole place had an uber cool, smooth, laid-back feel. Justin chose a table outside, the air was still thick with warmth and being outside allowed them to enjoy the music without being overwhelmed by it. As soon as they sat down though, a light breeze kicked up. Justin immediately took off his black zip up and put it over Allie's shoulders without her even having to ask or so much as shiver to indicate that the breeze was chilling her. She smiled and looked up at him.

Her smile met his and he leaned in and kissed her cheek, "I'll be right back with our wine."

Allie was in a state of shock that after the way the past year had gone that she was now enjoying the soulful company of a man who treated her like a queen. Hadn't Shelby said something like this to her, that every woman deserved to be treated like a queen while every man deserved to be treated like a king? At the time Allie had thought the notion of queen and king-dom was a little too over-the-top idealistic, even for Shelby. But here she was now experiencing a man who made her feel like a queen, who was attentive and kind. Although, Allie felt like she was going to need to get clearer about what treating a man like a king entailed. The way Justin made her feel was so out of this world that she wanted to do whatever she could to show him how much she respected and admired him.

Allie checked her phone again. Shelby and Laney had sent multiple text responses back encouraging Allie to see how Tawna was presenting her with an opportunity for deeper healing. Laney reminded her that when someone shows up in one's experience it's either because they are mirroring back an aspect of one's self or are showing you an old vibration from childhood or previous traumas that were ready to be released.

This made Allie pause in deep thought. She couldn't see any aspect of herself in Tawna's behavior, but she did realize that Tawna's manipulation and inability to honestly speak her truth were flashbacks to her marriage with Marcus. Marcus loved to have his way and loved to talk about himself. Allie was happy to oblige him and just go with the flow. But she recognized now that this was one of the reasons why their marriage could not last.

It's not a true, supportive relationship if it's only about one person. It simply won't work – in any relationship, including friendships – if one person is always dominating and the other person is continually acquiescing their needs and desires. And now here with Tawna, Allie had applied her usual behavior of going along the best she could to "manage" the other person's emotional outbursts – however begrudgingly. It didn't work anymore though; the Universe was not going to allow Allie to continue this pattern. Instead it was blowing up bigger and bigger, and Allie was now forced to handle the entire scenario differently. Now, with no place to stay and no access to her clothes and personal items, Allie felt a weird un-groundedness, like she was spinning in a vortex that was terribly unfamiliar. She was going to have to handle this from a completely new perspective.

Shelby's text reminded her that when we can handle things differently, it can cause us to feel like we're in chaos, but in truth, every aspect of our body-mind-Spirit is actually recalibrating to the new way of being. Allie would never have stood up to Marcus the way she did with Tawna in the bathroom. She also would not have gotten to that place of compassion and seeing the truth of the situation. She just would have done whatever she could to bring the situation into harmony and to calm down the angry party. But this time she could not bring herself to do that. Her connection with Justin – although very new – meant far more to her than keeping the peace with Tawna (or anyone for that matter). She didn't know why, but simply meeting Justin had altered the course of her life.

It was then that Justin returned, two glasses of Pinot Noir in hand. "Deep in thought, huh? Things must have gotten a little nuts with Tawna?"

She smiled slightly. "Yeah, you could say that. What was your first clue?"

He looked up reflecting for a moment. "I'm not sure, but about 2 hours ago I felt this strong tug in my solar plexus," He placed his hand to his mid-abdomen, over his diaphragm. "And I just knew it had to do with you. Not quite like you were in trouble exactly but that something had gone down. I kept checking my phone and actually felt pretty relieved when I did get your text message to come pick you up. Otherwise, I was liable to drive up and down The Block looking for you." He smiled as he reached out his glass of wine to cheers her.

Allie loved how tuned in he was to her.

"Okay then, here's to you rescuing me, because you truly did." Allie lifted her glass.

Justin brought his glass up, "Well, here's to you rescuing me, because you have as well." As their glasses clinked, Allie's mind wondered how she could possibly be rescuing him. It didn't take long for a whisper inside of her to respond, saying that she was rescuing him from a life without her in it.

———

Justin clapped his hands together, rubbing them. "Okay, get to it lady, what went down tonight? Spare no details, I love a good cat fight."

Allie laughed. "Sorry to disappoint you, it was definitely not a cat flight. Although it was dramatic." Allie had been hesitant to tell him the full story of "choosing him" but Laney and Shelby assured her that nothing good could come from keeping secrets especially not from a man that she clearly had a strong and soulful connection with. If she did, it would set the entirely wrong tone for their relationship (if that's where they were heading…Allie's critical mind always found a way to poke holes in whatever was happening). And while Allie would have preferred to be the "I have it all together girl" – she realized that simply wasn't the case in this moment and it was better for her to own that rather than skirt around what was happening.

"So…" Allie said with a deep breath. "Tawna basically got very drunk and angry and told me I was not allowed to stay with her for the remainder of my trip."

"Because…." Justin's head dipped down as he said this, clearly aware this was not the easiest thing for her to share with him…

"Because…" Allie's head followed his. "Because she feels that I am choosing you over her and that this is a pattern in our friendship. As she was sharing this with me, I had this moment of clarity where I saw her little girl self in desperate need of love and attention and anything that felt like a slight to that was triggering her. And apparently there *has* been a pattern in our friendship where she has been triggered repeatedly. So, I definitely can access compassion for her, but I'm really not sure what to do with that. The human side of me wants to be angry at her for being so dramatic so that now I have to get a hotel, get a rental car, etc. It's fine, but it's frustrating. You know? I had been trying in my own desperate way to avoid totally upsetting her and having things blow up between us. But here I am."

Justin seemed to be taking everything in as Allie spoke.

"Allie…" he said carefully. "You don't have to get a hotel or a rental car. You can stay with me, I'll sleep on the couch and I'll take you back to the airport in two days. It's really not a big deal. And then, we can spend more time together while we're at it." A smile beamed across his face.

Allie giggled internally. Men are so wonderful, she thought to herself, they hear a problem and they just dive right in and solve it.

"Justin, that is very generous of you, but…."

"Allie, I won't take no for an answer, so you're really wasting your breath here," he said smiling.

"Your couch is a loveseat – you won't even fit on it!"

"True, but what I am trying to say is that either way, we'll work it out. Ultimately if you want to get a hotel room, of course, do it, but I want you to know you don't have to." He leaned in, placing his hand on hers gently. "Okay?" His eyes locked into hers and Allie felt everything spin around her. This man was truly rocking her world.

Allie couldn't keep her focus off of his words that "we'll work it out." It had been so long since she had been part of a "we," since she had even thought that being a "we" was possible. She and Marcus had been so separate for so long – him immersed in his self-care routines, his therapy, his job, his friends that she couldn't even remember a time he had said, "we'll" do anything.

She leaned in to meet Justin, letting her lips intentionally come together with his, her hand on the back of his head, his hand gripping her thigh. She wanted to show him how she felt about him, she wanted her body to show him how he made her feel. Their tongues glided smoothly over one another's, their breath picking up pace, Justin's hand squeezing her tighter, her hand pulling with need at his neck. She imagined his strong hands running up and down her naked body and she shuttered. It was way too soon for her to be thinking about having sex with a man she met a few days ago, but her body didn't know the difference, her body wanted him.

"Justin," she breathed as she pulled away. "You are amazing," she allowed her eyes to look at him softly and his eyes were still closed taking her in.

With his eyes still closed he replied, their foreheads pressed together. "Being with you makes me amazing Allie. I've never experienced this before…" his voice trailed off.

"Neither have I," Allie breathed. "Neither have I."

Their lips found one another again and as his lips and tongue danced with hers Justin breathed into her mouth as his other hand held her face, "Stay. With. Me."

———

Any defenses Allie might have had up before about whether or not to get a hotel room or stay with Justin dissolved. Nervously he fumbled with the key to his home as Allie stood beside him while visualizing that she was tapping Cortices. Was she going to have sex with him? Would she ever see him again? Were they on the path to love and relationship? Her ability to not fast-forward into the future was long gone. From there, Allie's brain attempted to answer all of the questions while it brought up even more questions to be answered. As she continued to tap Cortices visually she noticed her brain's fast-paced "gotta figure it out" over-activity began to slow. By the time Justin's door opened she felt re-connected back to the now moment that was right in front of her.

"And here we are...my humble abode," Justin pronounced.

Allie let out a gasp, slapping her hand to her mouth. "What the hell did you do to this place?" She was in utter shock. Justin's place now resembled one of the most organized and clean homes she had ever seen. "And when did you have time to do this? I thought you've been with clients and the party..."

He placed his arm around her waist and pulled her into him kissing her right ear softly, nibbling on it ever so gently. "Well, you know, I want to make sure my lady feels comfortable at my place."

Allie turned to look at him. "Did you have some kind of intuition that Tawna was going to kick me out of her condo?"

He shook his head. "Not consciously, no. But I did have a strong intuition that I better get this place looking good or I might lose you forever." Justin looked intensely into her eyes. "And I definitely do not want that."

Allie wasn't sure what exactly Justin meant but her brain went to work on it, trying its best to decipher what he was saying. His lady? Forever? Lose her? With the trauma-drama earlier in the evening with Tawna, it was entirely too much for Allie to mentally process. Besides, she would have plenty of time for that later – hadn't Justin reminded her of this a day before? So, instead she did what any hot-blooded, intuitive woman would do – she grabbed his arm and pulled his body into hers. His hand reached up to hold her face, as he moved in to kiss her passionately. His body began to press more firmly into hers, backing her up against his living room wall.

Allie let out a surprised gasp as her body felt the wall behind it (she hadn't seen that coming!) and Justin's body pressed more deeply into hers.

His lips moved to her neck as his hands moved her arms up the wall, above her head. Their fingers entwined as he found her ear, plunging his tongue inside in a way Allie imagined he would plunge other parts of his body into hers, and it drove Allie wild. She let out a moan as she arched her pelvis into his. Now he had done it, she could not hold back and her hands instinctively started unbuttoning his shirt feeling the smoothness of his chest, digging her fingers into his flesh to let him know her need.

"Oh Allie," he whispered into her ear. "I want you."

She licked his ear, sucking on the lobe and surprising herself as she whispered back, "I want you too."

His hands slid down to her shirt as he pulled it up and off of her, revealing her lacy black bra, her large D-size breasts filling out the cups of the bra perfectly. Allie struggled to remember if she had the sense to wear the matching black lace thong panties and breathed a sigh of relief when the image of putting them on in the morning appeared.

Justin's eyes widened and met hers as he cupped her breasts with his hands.

"God, I love how you touch me," she moaned with pleasure.

"God, I love how you feel," he moaned back, moving back to her neck and ear, Allie unable to keep her hands still as she reached into his pants, eager to unzip them and discover more of him.

Suddenly, she heard a familiar tune that sounded like the mambo; it quickly escalated in sound and grew louder by the second.

"What the hell?" Justin said pulling back and moving around.

"Oh my god," Allie said, as she realized it was coming from the floor near them where she had dropped her purse. "Why the hell didn't I turn that off?"

"Oh, just leave it," Justin said as he resumed his position, licking and kissing her ear and neck.

Just as Allie began to sink her fingers into his firm ass, the mambo tune started up again, seemingly playing more loudly.

"Oh for god's sake," she said.

This time it was Justin who seemed more concerned.

"Maybe it's an emergency?" he offered.

Allie pondered the possibility for a moment but had trouble thinking of anything that could be more significant than what they were doing right then and there. Justin unhooked himself from her and grabbed her purse. He held it out to her, "Here sweetie, see who it is."

Allie grabbed the phone and rolled her eyes as she saw Tawna's name and photo flash on the phone. She showed it to Justin. "Soooo not worth interrupting us." As she went to push the "ignore" button, somehow she pushed "answer" and Tawna's high-pitched voice penetrated the room. Loud music blared in the background and Allie looked up at Justin horrified.

"So Allie, I'm sure you're with your new boyfriend who I'm also sure you'll be broken up with very soon like as soon as you get back to Oregon, but I just wanted you to know that your shit has been left at the front desk of my condo complex. Peace out!" With that Tawna hung up.

Allie looked up at Justin again. "I am so sorry. I meant to hit 'ignore' and somehow I answered it."

"Maybe some part of you wasn't ready to continue this?" Justin asked curiously.

"Maybe...but if so, it was 100 percent unconscious. I swear. I am so sorry."

Justin came over to Allie leaning her back up against the wall. "Are all of your friends this crazy?" he teased. "Cuz that girl is nuts. Either way though, let's go get your stuff...I mean shit. Who even says that?"

Allie giggled, pulling him back to her.

"I don't want to go anywhere just yet."

———

Before she knew it Justin had picked her up, scooping her up into his arms and carrying her into his bedroom. He laid her gently on the bed and then looked at her, his shirt still off and said, "Don't move." Allie followed his instructions and watched as he moved forcefully and with intention to light several candles around the room, and then put on some music. She was surprised by his music choice but also loved it at the same time. As The Cure's "Close to me" played softly in the background, Justin made his way back to the bed.

Allie lay on the bed, propped up on her elbows watching him. She loved that he took the time to create a romantic ambiance for them before they moved into whatever might be next. She wanted him desperately but at the same time wasn't sure if she was ready to have sex with him. She knew that once a man penetrated her, they were bonded in a way that transcended other casual romantic encounters. Not only did sexual penetration serve as a contract between two bodies, it also opened her up to receiving energetically from him. She had no way of knowing what this energy would entail, but she knew she needed to feel not only closer to Justin emotionally but she needed to know more about who this man truly was before she allowed him to enter her. Her body, her yoni, was a divine conduit to greater love and connection and despite how much her body was screaming for Justin she couldn't surrender to her desire for penetration just yet.

Fortunately, Justin either intuited this or was on the same page with her because when he came to the bed, he crawled behind her, wrapping his arms around her allowing his naked chest to press into her naked back. Allie sighed deeply as she felt the energy from his body soothe and envelop her.

"As much as I would love to make love to you I also want to take things a bit slower until we've decided what we'll do once you go back home. Is that okay?"

Allie turned to face him. "I was thinking exactly the same thing Justin. I really want to feel you in every way, but I also know penetration is such a big commitment energetically and spiritually, and I'm not sure we're ready for that."

Justin placed his hand on Allie's face and kissed her, slowly and with purpose.

"But that doesn't mean we can't connect in other ways," he whispered as he looked deeply into her eyes.

"My thoughts exactly," Allie replied.

"You see, I was thinking," Justin continued. "That maybe I could stroke you and that you could tell me what felt good and what you wanted more of." He began moving his hand down to unbutton her jeans. "And you could focus on the stroke and how good it feels, letting yourself sink further and further into it."

Allie had never been stroked so intentionally. She felt the heat coming off of Justin's hand as he unbuttoned her jeans and slid his hand carefully into her panties and to the top of the hood of her clitoris.

"Is this okay?" Justin whispered.

"Yes," Allie sighed as she arched her pelvis and pulled down her jeans, sliding both them and her panties off.

"Thank you," he whispered. Then he slowly moved his finger down to her clitoris and began lightly stroking it. Allie immediately felt the electricity and pleasure moving throughout her body, as she began to rock her pelvis slightly to meet his finger in the exact place she wanted it.

"You can relax your body Allie," he whispered. "Tell me where you want me to touch you, you don't have to move to adjust."

This was brand new to Allie but she loved taking instructions from him. After spending her whole life making all the plans and giving directions it felt so good to surrender to this man's tender guidance.

"Move down just a little bit," Allie breathed.

Justin adjusted "There?" and Allie cried out in pleasure.

"Yes, yes, yes," she repeated.

"Good, now breathe inhaling through your nose bringing the breath from your yoni up your spine and then exhale out your mouth letting the breath travel down the front of your body and back to your yoni."

Allie immediately began the breathing and noticed that as she did her yoni seemed to open up further as her legs butterflied open even more. She felt for the first time as though she was a flower that was opening up like never before. The sensations coursing through her yoni were also different than she had experienced before, they were somehow deeper – deeper inside of her, more filled with pleasure and a sense of expansion. Allie couldn't believe how wet she was and how present she was able to be, by placing her focus on Justin's finger and cycling her breath. She could feel Justin's erection pressing into her, his pants still on.

"What...ha...about...oh...you?" Allie struggled to get the words out, the pleasure was so strong.

Justin kissed her ear and whispered. "It turns me on so much to give you pleasure like this. You don't have to do anything."

Allie couldn't believe it, but she was so in the flow of the wetness, pleasure and depth within her she didn't have the ability to argue. Normally she would want to make sure her man was taken care of and would never let herself receive pleasure solo like this. But not now, not with Justin. She felt herself opening up into her radiant feminine essence, her fullest feminine expression of surrender and pleasure even more as her yoni opened up further and deeper.

Justin naturally adjusted his stroke to go deeper into her introitus and Allie's legs spread deeper still. He would spend time with his finger deep within and then adjust back to her clitoris, the pleasure was overwhelming to her and she knew she would climax soon.

"Justin... ah... I'm... I'm... oh god... I'm going... to... come."

"Let yourself go, stay with the sensation, keep your focus on the sensation and let the climax take you over. I'm right here loving you," he breathed.

As he finished those words Allie felt the climax building, she followed Justin's instructions and let herself feel deeper and deeper into it. The waves of pleasure climbed and her moaning increased. Anytime her mind went to a thought of "you're being too loud, etc." she brought her focus back to the stroke. Finally, she could hold it in no more and the climax released, Allie breathed into it and felt the waves of pleasure spiral throughout her entire pelvis and down her legs. Her legs shook as she screamed, "oh my god, oh my fucking god!"

Justin continued with the pressure to her clitoris as she writhed in pleasure and the orgasm continued. "Oh my god, it just keeps going!" she screamed.

"Stay with it my love, let it take you away. I'm right here," he whispered to her. "You are so beautiful Allie," he said as he sucked on the bottom of her ear lobe.

"Oh, oh, it's soo much!" Allie could feel her body tensing up, as though she had reached her pleasure quotient.

"Keep breathing Allie, follow your breath."

Allie moved her focus back to her breath and noticed that the waves of pleasure softened. Justin moved his finger back to her introitus, stroking it more firmly. Allie's breath began to soften and she felt her breath relax.

She had experienced the longest, most intense climax of her life accompanied by several orgasms.

I just might love this man forever. Allie thought as she drifted off into bliss...

9

Allie woke up several hours later to find Justin's arms wrapped completely around her, their naked bodies pressed tightly together. She smiled. Being so close to him felt so damn good to her. Last night after her mega-orgasm-climax they cuddled naked for a half hour or so before they both fell asleep in one another's arms. Somehow they stayed that way the entire night.

She had wanted to pleasure Justin to show him how amazing he had made her feel, but he quietly explained to her that he didn't want their sexual relationship to ever be transactional. He gave to her because he wanted to and he wanted to enjoy the energy of that connection, taking the sexual energy that had been ignited within him and allowing that energy to fill his entire body as he pressed it into hers.

This was not something Allie had even heard of, but the way in which Justin spoke about his views on sexual intimacy within a relationship fully resonated with Allie. She had always longed for a daily sexual connection with her partner but often grew bored with the usual routine. She wanted to be able to cuddle naked some nights, give sensuous massages on others, be totally penetrated by him on still other nights, or provide him with oral pleasure whenever she felt the desire. But she had yet to experience a relationship where this kind of variety was something they could talk openly about and she often found herself in one of only a handful of sexual positions she and her partner had found to take them each to climax. She experienced the transactional pleasuring Justin mentioned – you make me come and I'll make you come. She often felt like sex was just one big race to climax and that felt very empty to her. She wanted more. And she had a very good feeling that Justin could be a man she could explore all of this more with.

As Allie lay there reflecting on their experience and the possibilities that lay before them, Justin began to stir. She could feel his erection growing and pressing into her. She arched into him so he would know she was waking up too. He pressed into her again, this time fully hard. Allie loved the feeling of him against her and couldn't believe how comfortable she felt with him. It was as though Justin had been in her life for a long time, when actually it had been mere days.

"Good morning love," he said gently in her ear.

"Good morning to you," Allie responded as she rolled over and into him. They kissed and he rolled onto his back bringing her on top of his chest, his arms wrapped tightly around her.

"You are amazing, you know that, don't you?"

She looked up at him, her eyes wide as she said gently in his ear, "Thank you. And I have to thank you for something else as well. Last night. You who took me to a place that I had never been before within myself or with a man. So, thank _you_."

He smiled and kissed her on the forehead, rubbing his hands gently down her back. "I've never had an experience like that before either Allie. I've read a lot about orgasmic meditation and Kundalini energy but I've never used the concepts I've read about with anyone. I cannot even tell you how much it turned me on to be a witness to you opening up in that way." Allie was looking at him intently as he spoke, and he locked eyes with her. "You are seriously the most beautiful woman I've ever met."

Allie felt something within her heart open and expand, like the love she was experiencing with Justin was so big her heart needed to make more room for it. She leaned her head down and kissed him deeply.

"And just think, we're only getting started," she said as she gazed into his penetrating blue eyes.

———

While they made breakfast together and prepared to go pick up her luggage from Tawna's, Justin told Allie about orgasmic meditation, slow sex and Kundalini energy. Allie was awe-struck. She had never explored this area of sexuality and was soaking in everything Justin shared. Orgasmic meditation was a sexual/spiritual practice that a couple could perform a recommended three times per week. During it, the woman is naked from the waist down and lies on the floor with her legs butterflied open. The man is fully clothed and sits to her right side, one of his legs over her belly, his other underneath her. For 15 minutes he strokes the upper left quadrant of her clitoris while she focuses (much like what Justin did the night before with Allie) exclusively on the sensation of the stroke. Unlike their sexual escapade the night before though, the man's focus remains solely on the woman's clitoris and the sensations that he too is experiencing through their focused connection. It's recommended that the woman stay as still as possible and that the couple only exchange non-violent communication requests for adjustment in pressure and stroke. At 13 minutes an alarm sounds to let the couple know the orgasmic meditation (or OM as it's often referred to) is coming to a close. The man begins to make his strokes firmer to help ground the woman as she is coming down off of the orgasmic experience. At the 15-minute mark, the stroking ends and the man grounds the woman's energy by pressing the palms of both of his hands on her yoni (or vagina – but Allie disliked that word feeling that it and other words for the female genitalia were either inaccurate or had been used to diminish a woman. Yoni means "the source of life" and it felt like the purest terminology for her lady parts.). Then, the couple shares one sensation that they experienced during the OM that was an important moment for them.

As Justin made eggs over easy for them, Allie watched the intro OM video on YouTube and surprisingly felt her eyes fill with tears. She had never seen anything so beautiful, she had never experienced a man honoring a woman in this way – before last night's experience with Justin that is. Oming was a practice, so it was not recommended that the couple have sex right after, however one of the benefits of Oming is that the sexual energy stays strong between the couple so there is an increase in sexual activity outside of Oming. Also, since sexual energy is extremely healing, the practice is incredibly powerful for both the man and the woman. In fact, while reverse Oming (for the penis or lingam as it is called in Sanskrit) is also a practice, most men prefer the Oming practice exclusively with stroking a woman's clitoris – describing it as one of the most satisfying experiences they have ever had with a partner. Allie couldn't help but feel tremendous gratitude for Nicole Daedone in developing the OM practice as well as the men who shared in the videos about their experience with Oming.

Allie knew immediately that if Justin and she took things further she would love to have an OM practice with him. Almost right on cue, as the video was wrapping up, Justin came up behind her, his hands on her shoulders, kissing the top of her head and asked, "So, what did you think? Oh, and breakfast is ready."

Allie turned around and smiled up at him. "I teared up. It's amazing. I see how you gave me the Justin version of OM last night – which by the way if I haven't mentioned was simply the most incredible sexual experience of my life. And, I would love to share an OM experience with you at some point, if we see one another again, that is."

There. She said it. Neither of them had talked about what might happen in t-minus two days when she returned home. Would they see one another again? She had tried to keep it at bay but she couldn't hold it in any longer.

Justin grabbed her hands and pulled her to a standing position. "Of course we're going to see one another again. And of course we'll OM – either my version or the technical version –if it feels right to both of us."

Allie smiled. At least the conversation had been opened up. She placed both of her hands on his face, "Perfect. Answer. Now, let's eat, I'm starved!"

———

The next two days flew by. Allie and Justin did their best to maximize every minute together. She went with him to the beach to check in on work when he needed to while most of the time he was able to have people cover for him. This meant that they were able to spend time napping, cuddling, walking on the shoreline and talking about pretty much everything. Their sexual connection was building as well. Allie couldn't believe how much the breath work with the focus on sensation altered their experience together. They had tried it while Allie went down on Justin and he had a full body orgasm that left him completely speechless and Allie totally turned on, not to mention eager for further exploration. Bottom line for Allie – their connection on all levels – emotional, spiritual and sexual was magical. She had never known it was possible to connect with a man in the way they were connecting. And she had been married!

It was in the wee hours of the morning she was to head back home that they both knew they had to talk more about what was next for them.

She was lying on his chest, his arm around her – one of her favorite places in the world to be she had since decided – when he said it.

"Allie, I don't know what I'm going to do when you leave. I know it's only been five days but ever since I saw you in that yoga studio I knew I had to be near you. Now, life without you is not going to feel the same."

Allie felt tears welling up in her eyes. "I know, I've been playing a very good game of denial with myself just pushing out thoughts about 'what's next' after this incredible time with, you but I leave this afternoon so we've got to face it. Honestly, though, I can't even think about going back to what now feels like my old life. What are we going to do?"

Justin took a deep breath, allowing his diaphragm to fully rise along with his belly and then letting it all out in one large exhale.

"Well, we can do whatever we want to do. That's the good news. I'm pretty tied here at least until November when the season ends and business slows down. I know you have a great job where you are…it wouldn't be fair to ask you to move here…" he paused. "Maybe we can meet in the middle? Move to Arizona or Nevada or something?" Justin asked hesitantly.

"I know I've had the same thoughts – we've both created really great lives for ourselves where we live with successful careers and good support systems. One of us having to give it up is a lot to ask. Although I think that if this is what it feels like it is, it won't feel like either of us has to give anything up, right? Maybe a brand new location would do that for us?"

Justin was silent for a couple of minutes. Allie wanted to say more or try to find out what he was thinking but decided against it and let the silence remain.

"I love that theory Allie, I really do. And I really want it to be true for us…"

"Why do you think it's a theory?" Allie interjected, unable to help herself from sounding defensive.

"I've just, I've never seen a relationship where someone didn't have to give up something pretty significant for the relationship to work. That's scary right – cuz what if we're wrong?"

Allie had the same fears as well. But what was life if it wasn't about going for it – especially in the name of love she thought. She sighed, her hopeless romantic self was clearly back.

Justin continued, "My mom gave up everything for my dad. She focused on us kids, let go of her job as a nurse – that she loved – all to be a wife and mother. And honestly I don't think my dad has ever fully appreciated what she gave up for all of us. Sometimes I think I see a pained look on her face over this

— especially now that we're all grown. Like what could have been, you know? Now my dad plays golf all of the time and she volunteers and has lunch with her girlfriends. I'm not sure it was the right thing for her to do, even though I loved having her there as a kid. I would just hate to have you or I give up something that was so important to us and then have years of resentment or pain over the choices we made," he paused again. "Does that make sense?"

It did make sense, perfect brain sense that is. Allie could totally see Justin's logic in the whole situation, she was simply hoping for a more romantic response.

"I do understand," she whispered. "Unfortunately there's no way to know the future, so we can only make the best choices from our hearts as possible."

Justin kissed her forehead, stroking her hair softly. "And making a choice from our heart is really the only way to make any choice, isn't it?"

———

As they drove the 40 minutes to the Houston airport, tears streamed down Allie's face. Justin didn't speak and Allie did her best not to draw too much attention to the fact that she was having a serious emotional meltdown. A few minutes later he glanced over to ask about the temperature in the truck when he noticed that something was wrong, "Allie, are you crying? Are you okay? What's going on?" he turned his blinker on, signaling to pull off of the road.

"No, no — you don't have to pull over. I'm okay," she said hurriedly wiping the tears from her eyes.

But it was too late, he had pulled over. He put the truck in park and turned to face her. "Allie look at me, what's going on?"

Allie turned to him, tears filling her eyes again. "What if I don't ever see you again? I feel like you gave me this incredible gift, that our connection opened me up in ways I have never before experienced and now it's over. And we don't have a plan, we don't know when we'll see each other again or what will happen, and, I'm just, I'm, I'm freaking out a little bit about it…" her voice trailed off.

Justin's brow furrowed as he watched her speak. "I'm so sorry Allie. I wish I had the answers for you. I know we will see each other again, but I think we've got to see how we feel apart and step back into our lives and see what solutions might come to the surface. I realized this morning that I'm afraid. I'm afraid of not being with you, I'm afraid of what we both have to give up to be together, I'm afraid. This is a big deal to me. I mean Allie, I fell—" Justin stopped himself and cleared his throat, tears now filling his eyes. "I have never felt this way about anyone before Allie. It's totally spinning out my world. Please believe me, we will be together again – we will."

———

Allie heard Justin's words echoing inside her head as she walked to the airport gate to board her plane home. A plane she did not want to get on, but she knew she had to. She had considered extending her stay but she had a special project at work that she had to be there for and Justin had already put so much on the backburner during her five days there to be with her, he couldn't set aside more time either. She knew logically in her mind that he was right. They both needed to go back into their lives to see how things felt without one another and what possible solutions might emerge. But it didn't feel fully right in her heart. As she had walked away from his truck, tears slid further down her cheeks, the pain in her heart palpable.

Just then her phone rang. It was him.

"Miss me already?" she said playfully as she answered the phone.

"I do, actually, terribly, really," she heard him say.

"I know, me too. My heart is doing all sorts of strange things ever since I got out of your truck."

He was silent for a minute.

"I know, mine too. I'm feeling a lot of pain actually. Like…like a part of me is missing. I almost don't want to go back to the house and feel how empty it is without you."

Allie could feel the depth and the meaning of his words. It helped ease the nagging worry that something would happen and they would never see each other again. Maybe this man really *was* real, not just some romantic mirage that the Universe had gifted her with for a short period of time.

"Justin, thank you so much for expressing to me how you feel. It means so much to me. And I should have said this more during our time together, but thank you for everything you did for me – rescuing me from that nutty situation with Tawna, letting me stay with you, getting all of my stuff, taking me out to dinner, making me breakfast – you did so much for me and I can't even tell you in words how much it meant and means to me. You are truly an incredible man."

"Oh Allie, you're welcome, and of course. I would give you all of that times a million – anytime. So just know that – you can come here anytime and I'll do all of that – except for making the crazy friend rescue that is. I forbid you to have any more crazy girlfriends," he laughed. "But seriously, anytime. I've never met anyone like you before and I don't know that I ever will. *You* are incredible."

Allie had tears in her eyes all over again. Whatever the future held, she knew that her experience with Justin had changed her life forever.

———

"Okay, you have to tell us everything – and I mean everything," her four younger sisters practically said in unison. Laney and Shelby had made the trip down to the coast so that all five of them could be together to discuss what had transpired between Allie and Justin. Allie had text Laney and Shelby once she arrived back in Oregon with more of the deets after the Tawna drama, but they all agreed that what they truly needed was an in-person meet-up to properly give this turn of events what it was due. Alicia and Brittany were there as well and they had decided to meet up at Allie's to get all of the details. To prepare, each sister brought a bottle of her favorite wine and a couple of appetizers or a dessert.

That meant they had 5 bottles of wine (although as the preggers one of the bunch Shelby was sipping sparkling cider), a variety of artisan cheeses from Blue Heron, a local gift/wine/specialty store, and crackers (gluten-free for Laney), Shelby's favorite Paleo-inspired almond and cranberry cookies, hummus and veggies, a crock-pot of lil smokies (Alicia's specialty), peanut butter pie (Brittany's specialty), sweet potato chips, a roasted chicken, olives, figs and organic dark chocolate.

Allie and the girls made a picnic set-up on her living room floor, reserving the coffee table for the wine, as they all sat around in a circle.

"Well, I'd say we won't need to eat for at least 24 hours after this feast ladies," Allie noted.

The girls laughed and immediately began digging in to the food with Shelby taking the lead pouring everyone wine and kicking off the agenda for their gathering. "Okay Allie, so while we're getting started with the food and wine," she said as she handed a glass of Sokol Blosser 2011 Pinot Noir to Allie. "Why don't you get us started? We all know why we're here together, in person today. Allie has had a massive shift after one year of healing and we all want to support you Allie…"

"And we love to hear all of the gossip," Brittany chimed in.

Shelby, ever the big sister, threw her a playfully irritated look. "And yes, we can't stand it when something big is happening in one of our lives and we aren't all in on it – thank you Brittany for bringing that to our attention. But truly we want to not only hear all of the details – including this mega-orgasm you've referenced to Laney and me briefly…"

All the girls began to coo like schoolgirls, their eyes widening. "Ooohhh Allie – start there, start there!" Alicia yelled.

Again Shelby threw a sideways glance – she really did prefer to be in charge – over to Alicia. "*And* we know you'll share whatever you're comfortable with, so ready, set, go!"

Allie was laughing so hard. She loved these girls so much and honestly couldn't wait to share with them as much as they couldn't wait to hear from her. As she began to recount the details – including the intimate ones – of what transpired between her and Justin, she felt waves of energy moving through her body. She felt excitement radiating from her cells and she could feel that energy glowing from her body Apparently her sisters noticed it too.

Laney interrupted, "Girl, you must have been activating some serious Kundalini energy because I have *never* seen you look like this. You are literally radiating light from every pore in your body. I am going to get me some of this Orgasmic Meditation. It sounds delicious."

"It *is*. And Justin is so delicious that it really helps with the whole thing. We never made it to officially practicing OM, just our own version which I am more than happy to continue I might add."

"So…when are you going to see him again, how did you guys leave things?" Brittany asked, as an Aries she was always one who wanted to get right to the bottom line. The other girls nodded in agreement.

"Well…that's sort of the thing. We didn't set any formal plan. We agreed that our connection was out of this world and that we want to explore it, but we agreed that we needed to see what solutions popped in once we were back in our natural habitats. He has a really successful career in Shorespoint, and I have all of you and my awesome job here – we're not exactly eager to give up what we've worked so hard to build," Allie explained.

"But when it's love you aren't giving anything up; you are both receiving. In fact, both of your lives could be something a million times better than what you've created on your own Allie. That's what happened for me and Daniel. I had no idea my life could look like this," she said as she rubbed her belly. "We got pregnant right after we moved in together."

Just then Alicia mouthed "mirror incident" to all of the girls – making everyone roar with laughter at Shelby's story about how she had gotten pregnant – so overcome with desire while making out in front of a mirror Shelby and Daniel had thrown caution and birth control to the wind which led them right to where they were now.

Shelby rolled her eyes. "Is it still funny? Really?"

All of the girls nodded in agreement that yes, it was still the best story that any of them had on each other. Shelby couldn't help but laugh. It really was that good of a story, even now.

Alicia piped in again, "Although depending on where things go with Allie and Justin her orgasm story may take the cake…just sayin," she said as Shelby playfully swatted at her.

"Okay, but the point is – I had a job anyone would envy and a really good life," Shelby continued. "And now I have an epic life with the man I love and I'm loving being pregnant. Daniel's books are on the best seller lists, I make jewelry that I love when I'm not nesting for baby. My good life went to fantastic once I came together with my love. Even if I only get to sip apple cider while you lucky ladies down the wine. And…and – look at my friend Kathryn. Since she and Scott came together she has never been happier. They have a house – something she said she could never make a commitment to, she is writing for *The Huffington Post* and they hold energy healing events in their home *and* they just had their first six-figure year. She essentially has a life she never dreamed of now that she and Scott are together. I'm telling you ladies, the energy of being in relationship with the love of your life and allowing the creativity of that love to guide you – means you two get to create something that is above and beyond where you both are now."

Allie took in Shelby's words carefully. She couldn't deny it – she agreed wholeheartedly. But could she pick up everything she had built in Oceanside and move to Shorespoint to be with Justin? Is that what she really wanted to do?

Her sisters must have read her mind because Laney reached out and squeezed her hand. "Even though I totally agree with Shelby, it's still a tough choice to make. I think it's really smart that you two are taking time to let the Universe show you if things are meant to continue forward and if so what the solutions might be."

It wasn't like Laney to applaud a brain-only decision, but Allie knew she was simply trying to soothe her sister, not increase her fears.

"So, have you two been talking on the phone?" Brittany inquired, attempting to shift the focus a bit.

"Yeah, actually, we've been talking on Skype which has been really fun because we can see one another—"

Alicia interjected. "Oh, I know what that means – Skype sex!" The girls all burst into laughter, Alicia was always the one to take things back to sex. Sex and movie quotes tended to be her major contributions to their group time together – she was always the one making everyone laugh.

"Oh my god Alicia! No, we have not had Skype sex, although we have talked about it. We both agree we would probably just be laughing the entire time. It's still too detached via Skype. Although I will say I've been facilitating my own Oming sessions since I've been back this past week..."

"Well, don't tease us, tell us about that too!" Alicia said.

"It's not too complicated ladies – the focus is the same as OM and what Justin and I experienced – except that since it's only me, I place my focus solely on the stroke. If it's mid-day I set a timer for 15 minutes and—"

Alicia was at it again. "Mid-day? Damn girl your Kundalin-waa-waa or whatever Laney called it *is* in overdrive. Self-pleasuring mid-day? Well, that deserves a high-five!" Alicia reached over and high-fived Allie and then as the other girls began to laugh, high-fived them all. "Here's to mid-day self-OM ladies!" Everyone raised their glasses and cheered.

When Allie could finally catch her breath from laughing so hard she continued. "Yeah, it is pretty epic. I had like a 10-minute orgasm yesterday. It just kept going – the energy was moving throughout my entire pelvis, legs and into my belly – it was pretty mind-blowing. The tough part though is not going into fantasy about Justin. I started reading Nicole Daedone's book *Slow Sex* since I got back and it talks about the importance of the focus – which is what makes it like a meditation. It's hard not to pull Justin's sexiness into my stroking. But, even so, I'm having success."

"I'd say a 10-minute O is definitely a success," teased Alicia.

———

Allie couldn't help but hear Shelby's words echo in her mind as she washed dishes and the girls watched the latest episode of The Bachelor in the other room. Shelby described relationship and love as a creative process, one that transformed both people's lives into something much more than it was when they were single. She just couldn't imagine what her life would look like with them together in one location or staying apart. Nothing felt right.

She heard the girls laughing in the other room and smiled. Justin would love them and they would love him. She could see him here with her, coming up behind her while she washed dishes, kissing the back of her neck softly, whispering in her ear about what they would be doing once the girls left...

"Can't stop thinking about him can you?"

Alicia interrupted and Allie snapped her head to the left to look at her, her face red with guilt.

"Damn girl, we are gonna have to life flight your ass to Shorespoint if this goes on too much longer," Alicia teased. Allie smiled and nodded, and Alicia could tell that her sister was weighing the pros and cons of the situation carefully.

"I know it can't be easy after what you went through with Marcus to now have found love again, but so far away," Alicia said, joining her at the sink and taking over rinsing duties. "And even though I make fun of – well, pretty much everything – but more specifically Laney and Shelby's woo-woo-ness, you know as well as I do that everything works out the way it's meant to. If Justin and you are supposed to be together then no matter what, the way will be found for you two."

Allie looked over at Alicia and then leaned in and kissed her on the cheek.

"Ugh, god, you don't have to get all sentimental on me," Alicia said as she flicked water at Allie.

"I really do appreciate you trying to make me feel better sweetie. I know you're right and that thinking about it non-stop will only create more angst within me and won't bring any resolution to it. I just...I just always hoped I would feel love again, and I'm so excited it has happened. It seems a little cruel that it has to happen so far away from me."

"Who's so cruel?" Shelby waddled in, her hand rubbing her belly.

"Oh, no one – just God." Alicia cracked.

"Oh no, am I going to have to call up my guru Goddess bestie Kathryn to talk some sense into you two? What are you blaming God for now?"

Allie gave Alicia a look. "We're not blaming God, the Universe, Source or Spirit for anything Shelby. Alicia and I were just trying to understand why I would finally find love again, but have it be so far away." Allie didn't like the sound of her voice, it sounded heavy. It sounded a bit victim-y too. She knew in her heart that coming together with Justin wasn't happening *to* her. It was happening *for* her. She sighed. She really missed Justin and wished he was there to put his arms around her.

Shelby cracked a smile and said, "Well, that's an easy one to answer. It wouldn't be happening unless one or both of you were meant to make some very big changes. Make no mistake, the Universe does not provide accidents. You fall madly in love with a man that lives a couple thousand miles away from you, you're either supposed to live in Shorespoint with him or he's supposed to live here or you two are going to start over somewhere brand new. You are always being led. So, there, mystery solved."

With that she kissed them both on the head and waddled back to the living room.

10

A month and then another passed and Justin and Allie made the best use of their long-distance status as possible. Skype sessions, texting, emailing and even some phone sex made the time pass with ease. They didn't talk about the future; Justin had said that he didn't want them living for when they would see each other again. They agreed that when it was time to see one another again, they would know and they would make that move then. In the meantime, they would make the best of the distance and use it to enhance their already strong connection and see where it would lead them to next.

Daily communication with one another became a regular part of their life routines and Allie caught herself smiling for apparently no reason a lot of the time. She would even wake up with a smile on her face. She had forgotten how transformative the power of love was. How, like Shelby had said, when two people come together a creative life force energy takes hold that allows a whole new life to emerge.

Allie found herself no longer willing to engage in conversations at work that weren't positive. She reached out and volunteered for opportunities that would enhance her skill set and was signing up for trainings in the area of computer technician, simply because it interested her. Justin was seeing his business double over the previous year's income and they both knew this increase in success was because of the strong connection they shared.

"It really seems like I can't imagine a time you weren't in my life," Justin said one night as they chatted via Skype.

"I know; I feel the same way too. It's only been a couple of months and it seems like we have always been doing this. I can't believe how natural having you in my life – even from a distance – has been."

"I gotta tell you though Allie, this distance is tough. I really miss you most of the time." Justin sighed, putting his hands to his face. He suddenly looked stressed.

Allie sighed too. She was nowhere near knowing what they "should" do about their situation. Any time she thought about it, she noticed that she would end up with a screaming headache. She had to start carrying around a bottle of ibuprofen with her just in case a headache hit. Shelby kept telling her she needed to "feel her feelings" to find out what the headache was telling her (again) but Allie didn't have time for it. She chocked it up to stress and downed a few ibuprofen – which always did the trick.

Justin looked up at her and she thought she saw tears in his eyes. "I didn't want to have to tell you like this Allie, but…" he moved his hands through his blonde hair and sighed again and Allie felt her stomach tighten. She instinctively put her hand on her stomach and suddenly Laney's guidance to breathe from her belly, inhaling through the nose, exhaling through the mouth to release tension popped into her mind. Justin's pause was taking some time anyway, she needed to do something with the silence. What did he have to tell her that he didn't want to tell her? What could this be? Had something happened? She kept breathing into her belly, trying to ground herself for whatever was about to come next.

Finally, he let his hands drop in front of him and he looked into the screen and said, "I love you Allie." He said it fast and hard as though getting it out would make it easier. As if what he had to say needed to be rushed or he would lose the nerve to say it. "I know it's crazy to tell you like this – especially over Skype of all things – but I just had to, I had to tell you."

Allie sat looking into the computer screen shocked. It had only been two and a half months since they met. She and Marcus had waited almost a year before uttering those words to one another. If they started saying "I love you" now, then they would have to move forward with increasing speed. They would have to move soon; someone would have to relocate their entire life for the other. And then what? There could be resentments just like what Justin had mentioned before that could grow and fester if it wasn't the "right" move. And then before she knew it she would be sitting down to breakfast only to hear the words "I don't want this" being said yet again to her face. Allie's head spun, she opened her mouth to speak but couldn't say anything. She couldn't say it back. How could she say "I love you" now? If she said it back, they would be full throttle in the midst of what they were both working incredibly hard at avoiding.

"Whatever Allie, it's not like you have to say it back. I just had to tell you. It's been eating a hole in my stomach," Justin said.

"Thank you Justin," she said weakly – it was all she could get out.

Justin stretched his arms wide and yawned. "Well, I should probably get to bed." Allie could hear the tightness in his voice. But something inside of her wouldn't let her say more.

"Oh, okay. Yeah, I guess I'm feeling kind of tired too," she said, weaker still. She could feel a headache coming on already.

They said good night and Allie sat in her chair, the computer screen blank, a pounding in her head and in her chest. What in the world was wrong with her? Why couldn't she say "I love you?" She numbly stood up and walked into her bedroom, taking off her clothes as she got closer, crawling into bed, her head in her hands.

———

Allie was in bed for 3 days following her Skype love

conversation with Justin gone terribly, terribly wrong. Her headache took on epic size proportions, creating nausea and the inability to function properly. She couldn't even think it hurt so badly. Justin had text her the day after their conversation and she had told him she was really sick and couldn't talk, that she would call him as soon as her head stopped throbbing. She literally could feel nothing but the pain in her head.

By the third day, she called Alicia, she simply didn't know what else to do. Could she go to the doctor for a headache? Alicia came right over and was talking loudly on the phone when she came in.

"Oh my god, she is curled up in bed, the room is totally dark and her clothes are scattered everywhere. What do I do?"

"You lower your voice!" Allie hissed as she held her head.

Alicia moved the phone to the side of her mouth. "I didn't know what to do. I had to call Shelby and Laney. I've got them on a three-way call. I'm the baby sister, remember? You ladies take care of me. I have no idea what to do, I have to call in reinforcements. You know if we take you to the doctor they are just going to give you drugs that cause about 10 other side effects. Shelby and Laney are already quickly diagnosing you. Shelby wants to know what happened with Justin?"

"Justin? What does this have to do with Justin?" Allie was in no mood for a gossip chat, she just needed her head to stop hurting.

"Shelby says that you started getting bad headaches after you got back from Shorespoint – minus the one you got with Tawna, which was undoubtedly a precursor to this – because of the Justin stuff. So, give it up Allie, what's going on?"

Allie could barely think back. Recalling the information actually seemed to increase the dagger-like pain pounding throughout her skull. "He said he loved me on Skype."

Alicia gasped and reported this back to Shelby and Laney. "Yeah, totally," she said into the receiver. She looked back at Allie, now in a fetal position. "And what did you say?"

Allie couldn't believe she had to have this conversation

right now instead of being carried into the car and taken to the emergency room so she could be pumped full of awesome drugs that would take all of her pain away. But despite her desire to avoid the topic all together, the truth hit her. Like a Mac truck. Like the Mac truck that had clearly hit her head. She had said nothing. Her eyes hit Alicia's and Alicia knew. That was the beauty of the sister connection – sometimes there was no need for words. "She said nothing," she reported back into the phone. "Mm…hmmm, pretty sure you're right on that one." She looked back over at Allie. "How soon after this did the headache hit?"

It was too late; Allie knew what was happening too. This was no random headache. This headache had something massive to tell her. "Immediately," she whispered.

With that Alicia was set into action. She put Shelby and Laney on speaker phone as Shelby walked her through tapping Allie's Cortices. Laney began to guide Allie through a focus and release technique so that Allie could use her breath to begin releasing the emotions that were getting stuck in her head and not being processed by her diaphragm like they should have been so they could be released properly from her body.

"Focus in on the tension in your head Allie. Take a deep breath into it. Ask it what it wants to tell you."

The intensity of the pain had already diminished in severity just from Alicia tapping Cortices about half a dozen times in a row for her. She had no idea why it had not occurred to her to tap Cortices on herself for the past 3 days. It occurred to her it was most likely self-sabotage – something she was sure would surface from this impromptu healing session she was receiving from her incredible sisters. She did as instructed and when she breathed into the pain she heard all of the story, all of the swirling about how it couldn't be possible for two people to be in love so soon. About how if she even did love someone again he would probably just leave her like…like Marcus did! She said this part out loud without even realizing it consciously.

"What did Marcus do?" Alicia asked softly.

Laney picked right up on what was happening. "Leave her. That's what this is about. If Allie loves someone again that sets her up to be left again, like what happened with Marcus. She is terrified to truly feel these emotions because of the pain she has associated from her relationship with Marcus. So, rather than feel them they are getting trapped in her head, where she is swirling them around incessantly and which has been creating massive pain in her head. And…" Laney directed her comments now more specifically to Allie. "Popping that ibuprofen every time you got a headache instead of listening to this story that your body was trying to give you, just repressed it more and more which led to this huge debacle. You have to listen to your body, Allie, you can't avoid and deny the truth that it needs to share with you."

Allie could feel movement in her head as the pain lessened. Then Shelby piped in. "My BodyTalk practitioner is doing a remote session on Allie now to support this headache in fully releasing. The emotional focus and release work we just did moved a lot. She is emailing me the session as soon as she finishes Allie and I'll forward it to you. She texted me to let me know she started it. I emailed her a photo of you and gave her the emergency scoop. And it's my gift to you Allie so don't worry about payment – she costs some bucks, but she is worth every penny – that's how good she is. How you doing over there?"

Allie's eyes had been closed as she felt massive amounts of energy move from her head and then down into her heart and through her torso. "I'm, I'm feeling a lot of energy movement right now."

"In your head or elsewhere?" Laney asked.

"She's using her hands to gesture to her heart and torso Laney," Alicia piped in. Allie felt almost trance like and couldn't speak.

"Since the session is happening now it's probably best Alicia if you go in the other room and let's just give her space to receive it. She's going to be okay now," Shelby said.

Alicia walked to the other room and as she did Allie could

hear her say, "How in the hell is she feeling what that BodyTalk lady is doing when she isn't even here touching her? This is some crazy shit ladies."

Allie felt herself crack a smile. Three days in bed with pain and still Alicia could make her smile. Allie instinctively anchored back to some deep breaths, remembering what Laney had guided her through. She now felt the pain in her stomach and she placed her hand there, breathing into it. *What do you want to tell me?* She asked.

I am sick of trying. I am sick of protecting. I am sick of feeling sad that Marcus left. I am sick of wanting a love that I'm too afraid to have.

Tears began streaming down Allie's face.

I am sick of pretending like it's okay to love a man and not be with him. I am sick of keeping this part of myself hidden from everyone, including me.

With that, the tears began to pour down her face as she sobbed into her pillow, turning into a ball, feeling the cramping in her stomach and the release of tension in her head.

I don't want to live like this anymore Allie. She heard her body say. *We need to be free. We need to be free to love. We need to stop caring that who we love will leave. Maybe they will leave. Maybe they will stay. But what matters is the love. You have to let yourself feel the love Allie. That's why you're here. Don't you know that? You are here to love. It is the only thing you're here to do. That's why you were depressed for a year, that's why you've been in bed for 3 days in pain — you haven't been doing the very thing you are here to do. To love. With abandon. With joy. With openness.*

Allie sobbed and sobbed as her body continued on.

We need your cooperation now Allie. We need you to listen to us and trust us. Because if you don't our message will have to get louder and louder and usually the only way you can hear it is through body pain. You need to do things differently Allie. You need to make changes. You need to allow love into your life.

She wasn't sure how long she laid there for or what all her body had shared. But as she heard the messages, she felt movement throughout her whole body. Her stomach stopped cramping and by the time Alicia came back in and sat on the bed with her, she could raise her head up.

"Hi," she said to Alicia. "Whatever just happened was unbelievable."

Alicia grabbed a tissue from the Kleenex box on her nightstand and patted her face. "Shelby said you might have a good cry. How do you feel now?"

Allie noticed that her head was only a dull ache and that her whole body felt exhausted, although not in pain, but as if it had been holding so much tension for so long that it had finally been able to let go of. Alicia didn't wait for her to respond and began tapping Cortices again on her. "Shelby said I should tap a few more times and then let her know how you are doing. She also said you are going to need to drink a lot of water and that you'll be pooping a lot."

Right on cue, Allie's stomach began making loud gurgling noises. "Oh my god, this stuff is no joke."

"I know, I'm pretty much a believer now and I didn't even have the session," said Alicia. "Can I help you to the bathroom?"

"Yeah, I think I'm going to need it. Three days of no food and pain along with whatever magical healing I just now received has made me a little weak."

With that, her little sister, a sister she remembered carrying as a small baby, helped her out of bed and into the bathroom. Allie couldn't help but feel incredibly blessed.

———

It was a couple more days before Allie felt the life within her fully return. She hadn't realized how much energy she had used every single day in protecting herself after the break-up with Marcus. Falling for Justin in the way that she had, had flooded her system with love but also a reactionary protection method based on her limiting beliefs that any man she loved would leave her just as Marcus had.

She had followed Shelby and Laney's guidance to the letter. Tapping Cortices hourly, drinking 3-4 liters of water a day, and using the focus and release breath process to tune into her emotions and hear the messages they were trying to give to her. She also had Shelby schedule a follow-up remote distance session with the BodyTalk practitioner who had facilitated – from over a hundred miles away – such a powerful healing for her. She never, ever wanted to experience pain like that again. And she knew feeling her feelings was going to be the key to making sure her body never had to be that dramatic in its communication to her.

Surprisingly she and Justin had not been able to connect since all of this had occurred. He would call and leave a message when she was sleeping and then she would try and call and would miss him as well. They traded texts and she let him know that something big had happened – that she had experienced a miracle healing from breath and energy work – but she hadn't gone into intimate details. Justin had responded with interest although he had no direct experience with this kind of radical healing. Even so, he was supportive in his texts and messages, although there seemed to be a feeling of distance between them.

By the time she felt like herself again a week later, she knew they needed to have a real conversation about what had happened. She knew that her reaction to his "I love you" had been based solely on her fear and her story about what love meant after her break-up with Marcus. She knew it wasn't fair to Justin and she knew that from his tense response, he was hurting too. But talking about these kinds of sensitive subjects was not exactly her forte.

So, when she got his voicemail for the fifth time – after two months of rarely any missed connections – she was frustrated and feeling rather desperate to have a real conversation with him.

"Hey Justin," she began the message, an edge to her voice. "This is Allie. You might remember me, you know, Allie Strauss. We met once. It was really awesome. And then well, and then, it's been awhile. So if you do remember me and you'd like to talk, please give me a call back."

———

Three days later and still no return call, text or email from Justin.

"Three days Shelby, I am freaking out," Allie practically screamed into the phone. "Not even a text message. I fucked this one up royally."

"Breathe Allie," Shelby said. "You are not in control of this thing anyway. Remember that. Now, what exactly did you say in the voicemail – something like do you remember me?"

"Yeah, something like that. I was trying to be, I don't know, cute, funny, clever…"

"In a voicemail after he had told you he loved you and you did not reply and then proceeded to make yourself so sick – through your lack of ability to feel your feelings I would like to remind you – that you decided a cute or clever 'maybe you remember me?' voicemail message was appropriate?"

It wasn't like Shelby to be snarky. That was usually Alicia or Brittany's job. But being practically ready to give birth at any moment would do that to a woman. Besides, Allie knew she had every bit of it coming.

"Can you send me the BodyTalk lady's email address Shelby? I'm going to need to book weekly sessions I think. I totally sabotaged everything even after realizing the feelings were all my deal and not even really about him."

Shelby sighed. "I'm sorry for snapping at your honey. We all go through this stuff. Having your husband tell you he doesn't want to be married to you anymore creates serious trauma in the body. It's understandable. I just need to get this kid out of me so I can breathe and then I can do a better job of holding space for you. Hang on Allie –"

Allie could hear Daniel in the background, kissing Shelby and telling her how radiant she looked.

"Daniel just made the number 1 spot on the best seller list Allie! Can you believe that? We've got to celebrate!"

"Oh my god Shelby – that's amazing! Give Daniel a high-five for me, will you and yes get to celebrating. Thank you so much for listening. I so appreciate you. You saved my ass when that headache hit me and you have helped me so much.

Thank you Shelb. I love you."

"It's gonna be okay Allie. It really is. Just keep feeling your feelings and keep on with the BodyTalk, things will shift. And I love you too sis."

———

And shift they did. Into a void of nothing-ness from Justin. Allie tried texting and calling again, but no response. She had had her second shot at love and she had blown it straight to hell.

"If there was a hell that is," Alicia had no problem pointing out that Allie's self-induced pity-party was straight up bogus over lunch at the Pelican Pub & Brewery. "So, you met an amazing man. You OMed, you had a 10-minute orgasm, it was two months of awesome, and it didn't work out. It's okay. But you can't use it as an excuse to launch yourself into a pool of despair. I mean, look at me? I date whomever I want, whenever I want and I'm perfectly happy. Suck it up, sista, no one likes a whiner. You can't just break down cuz a boy isn't showing up the way you want him to. Let it go. There are a billion kick-ass fish in the man sea." Alicia smiled at her, seemingly proud of herself for being the one to hand out the sister advice. With that, she took a big bite of her bacon burger, all the while still smiling at Allie, ketchup and mustard slathered all over her face.

Allie couldn't help but laugh, at least a little bit. First, because Alicia was so ridiculous and secondly, because she was so right. This was part of life. It was part of dating. Sometimes it worked, sometimes it didn't. She *did* need to suck it up and at the prompting of Alicia she needed to do so quick style if she wanted to keep from spending a year of her life being in a self-indulgent depression funk as she had spent the previous year. Thankfully the BodyTalk was helping to keep her from getting *that* dramatic. She felt terrible about the entire turn of events. But she did her tapping and her breath work and her BodyTalk practitioner even had her journaling. She had practices, she had support, this wasn't like what happened with Marcus. She was a different person now.

Allie took a long, slow sip of her ice tea as she let Alicia's hilarity and truth sink in. She watched as a couple in the far corner of the restaurant held hands and smiled at one another. She felt the chill of the ice tea and of her current life situation move through her. She shifted her focus over to Alicia who was still thoroughly enjoying her decadent burger. Allie smiled. She loved her little sister.

"I can always count on you to give it to me soft and sweet Lish," Allie joked. "I know you're right, I simply can't believe I could have that intense of a connection with a man and he could blow me straight off. Like not even a break-up text – worse, just dead air."

Alicia turned to her in disbelief. "He told you he loved you. And you said nothing. To preserve any shred of self-respect he has, what else could he do? You're not the victim here Allie. No one is. It's just one of those things that happens in relationships."

Again, Alicia was hitting her with the hard truth. Allie shook her head. How could she have said nothing? How could she have gotten so stuck in her head? How could she have been so afraid that she shut down? She was falling deeply in love with Justin but it wasn't something she could even admit to herself, let alone him. And now it was too late. She wanted to be tough like Alicia suggested, but her heart had softened so much to Justin that it was going to take her awhile. Her heart wanted what the couple in the far corner of the restaurant had – or at least what she imagined they had – everlasting love.

———

"Here's what you do, you communicate with him energetically. So, he's not available for direct communication? That's just fine. Call in his Soul and talk to him that way," Laney suggested this matter-of-factly as she sucked on a popsicle on Allie's back porch on a warm Tuesday summer afternoon.

"Wait – I do what now? I communicate with his Soul? How would I do that?"

Despite Allie's best intentions another month had passed and she still could not stop thinking about Justin. He was in her dreams at night and in her thoughts during the day. She had almost sent him a dozen more texts and emails but had managed to stop herself. It was clear that it was over for him, but it wasn't over for her.

"Make it like a ritual Allie. Light candles, tap your Cortices, quiet your mind and then call in his Soul. Once you feel his energy there, talk to it – tell him what you think and how you feel. Ask him to contact you. Then, see what happens. See what he says back. It will either bring things to completion so you can move on or perhaps there is more for you two to work out together and he'll come back in."

Allie looked at Laney sideways, but was still intrigued. What was the worst that could happen?

"And if you don't believe me, ask Shelby, she'll back me up on this. Everyone and everything is energy. I've had friends who have had complete closure this way in a relationship. They worked it all out in the Soul realm and then nothing more needed to be done. That's what dreams are doing essentially as well – working out what we're unable to in the 3D realm."

––––––

It was almost dark out when Laney gave Allie a big hug and left to head back to Portland after a long weekend at the Coast with her and the girls. Immediately, Allie began to marinate more on Laney's Soul ritual suggestion to connect with Justin. And she realized that she didn't need to call Shelby to verify the validity of the practice. She felt instantly when Laney had suggested it that it was something she needed to try. With the way things had gone, she didn't feel like she had anything to lose. Justin wasn't talking to her anyway, and who knew – maybe his Soul wouldn't talk to her either – but she had to find out.

She turned on her gas fireplace and lit candles all throughout her living room. She put on her favorite nighty, a soft pink chemise with spaghetti straps, lace covering her breasts and along her thighs. She sat cross-legged on her overstuffed couch and began to tap Cortices. She took several large deep breaths, inhaling through her nose and exhaling through her mouth. She closed her eyes and softened her breath, intuitively placing one hand on her heart and one hand on her yoni.

Then, Allie let herself imagine that Justin was in front of her. As if he was right there with her. For some reason, she felt words tumbling out of her mouth, *"Justin please come to me now."*

All of a sudden she felt the air in her condo stir and chills began to run up and down her body, causing the hair on her arms to stand on end. She could feel him. Her mind wanted to jump in with "what's happening?!" but she pushed it aside. It was like he was right before her, although not the physical body that he was in, but his essence was before her. She could almost smell him, taste him, reach out and touch him it was so tangible, so real.

She kept her eyes closed so that she could feel him more strongly; she sensed that if she opened her eyes it would pull her out of the vortex of whatever she was connecting with.

She began to speak, *"Justin I want you to know how sorry I am about how I handled things when you told me you loved me. It brought up so much fear within me and I wasn't able to speak to you from my heart. The truth is that I was falling madly in love with you and until that moment I didn't realize how terrified I was to open my heart fully and experience true love again. Our connection exceeded the connection I had with my husband by leaps and bounds and the ending of that relationship nearly broke my heart in two. I couldn't wrap my mind around what might happen between us if I opened my heart to you in ways that I had never experienced before. I'm so sorry if I hurt you. I want you know that my response or lack thereof was all about me, it had nothing to do with you or any way that you were not showing up for me. I am so blessed that we were able to come together in this life. I feel like having the experience with you and our connection has made all the difference in my life. It's as though our connection brought me back to life – to a life that included truly loving another."*

Tears began to stream down Allie's face.

"And I miss you. I miss you every day. I don't know what words I could use or what I could say that could help you understand the power and the impact you have had on my life. It is unlike anything I've ever experienced before. And to think that somehow I hurt you and caused our connection to stop...it just kills me Justin. I have spent the past month that we have not been communicating delving deeper into my heart to learn who I am and how I love in deeper ways. As I began to do that I began to see our life together. Mornings waking up next to one another, breakfast together, long walks along the water, conversations that went into the night, playing and laughing with one another, deep sexual connections unlike anything we have experienced before. I could feel it. I could feel my heart open – burst open really – as I let myself go to the all of the places I wouldn't let myself go before. It's like my heart was just waiting for me to sink into it and ask it what was possible. And I could feel you and our life together. I could feel that I would come to be with you and it would be perfect for both of us."

Allie took a deep breath; she knew there was more she needed to share. She needed to go deeper. She could feel Justin's energy pressing into hers, almost as though their energetic bodies were coalescing. She knew he needed her to go deeper, to share from the places she had not shared with anyone previously. Allie tapped Cortices, with a focused intention on connecting ever more fully with Higher Consciousness to allow her to speak what was on her Soul, things even she didn't fully understand but knew was within her and needed to be shared.

"After taking a break from the stroking practice, I resumed it and delved into a 10-day immersion. As I did this, I began to notice that my yoni had wisdom to give me, messages for me that would support me and support us in moving forward. She whispered secrets of long ago, secrets and knowings that I could not have anticipated. And Justin, it is truly amazing the wisdom that is locked inside of our bodies. The ancient yet so present wisdom that can guide us to everyone and everything we are meant to experience. I didn't know if I should connect with you in this way but when I asked, I heard that it was the most powerful ritual I could partake in with you. That my body needed/ needs you. That you are the key to the lock within me. That when you enter me, I am opened up to a greater part

of myself that I cannot access without you. That when you enter me, you connect to a deeper, more expanded you that is impossible for you to access any other way. That the wisdom in our bodies knows what we need far more than the mind knows. That saying a body needs another to unlock its greatest potential is not popular amidst a culture that revers independence above all else. But that it is the deepest truth never told.

That we come together — divine feminine and sacred masculine — to create beyond worlds, to merge into a harmony that is impossible to experience as an individual. That our desire to know another on the deepest levels goes beyond marriage and the mainstream relationship paradigm. That our deepest growth comes from harmonizing and entwining ourselves with one another while still feeling the strength of our soul within. This is how we experience true oneness. When you enter me, you unlock the highest potential within me and yourself. That together we bring the deepest, most powerful alignment to our souls and this radiates everywhere to everyone we meet and everyone who encounters us. This is a sacred coming together, a partnership that is beyond words. A partnership beyond worlds really. And can you believe it Justin that my yoni had all of this to share? That we have the opportunity to create a partnership unlike anything you or I have ever known, even beyond what anyone around us may have experienced? And that the power of our coming together would ripple out and impact so many of those around us?"

Allie's whole body was shaking now. She could feel energy swirling around her, the crown of her head felt as though energetic laser beams were penetrating through her. She could feel joy all around her. It was as though speaking these words was opening a portal into something that her conscious mind could not fully understand. Hell, she didn't even know those words existed within her. It was like she was giving words to something she knew, but only had remembered just then. Intuitively, Allie placed one hand on her womb, another on her yoni. She breathed into these powerful centers within her allowing her exhale to ground her into her root, her true center. The place where more wisdom than she could have imagined lived.

As she did this Allie started to hear something, it was soft, like a whisper, but it was swirling around her, it was being breathed into her, she couldn't understand where it was coming from but she knew it was coming from another realm, the realm she was accessing through this process. She could not feel the separation of energy of her and Justin, it was within her and all around her.

Yesss...Yessss...Yesss...Yes

The power of the yes caused her entire body to shudder with ecstasy. Her mind tried to grasp on – who was saying "yes" and where was it coming from? But the deep wisdom of her body shushed it away. She breathed into the yes and felt waves of orgasm penetrate her body, from the tips of her toes to the top of her head. She kept her hands on her womb and yoni as the waves of pleasure coursed through her.

Yess...Yes...Yes...Yesssssssssssssssss

Allie was on fire, her body responding to a pleasure that was both new and ancient. A pleasure that had been known and felt before when conscious, connected Souls united as one. But this was a newly summoned forth pleasure that was coursing through Allie's body. It was beyond her stroking practice or even Oming. Justin was with her, he was flowing through her as she flowed through him. They were truly one and it was the most ecstatic experience of her life.

Allie moaned with pleasure, breathing into the energy that was running through her. Then, just as effortlessly as it had begun to flow through her, it slowly began to subside, the exhale of her breath grounding her back into her body as the energy dissipated. Allie felt one last powerful breath move through her and then she felt a deep sense of calm within her very being.

"Justin?" she whispered.

Silence.

"Justin, I love you." She said clearly and with purpose.

I...Love...You. She heard in a low voice, barely above a whisper.

A single tear released from her left eye, and a smile spread across her face. Carefully she opened her eyes. Her living room was restored to its natural setting even though she felt like she had been transported to another place and time during the ritual. A place that was seemingly a million miles away from where she currently was. But now she was back home, candlelight dancing around her, the fireplace purring its comforting purr. Her smile spreading throughout her entire body.

Suddenly, she knew everything she needed to know.

The ritual was complete.

———

It was over a heavenly piece of chocolate chip cheesecake at her favorite restaurant Rosanna's that the topic of Justin returned. Allie hadn't talked about the ritual with anyone. It wasn't because she was keeping it a secret but because it felt like something she wanted to savor for a while before she shared it with anyone else. She could still feel the energy move around her crown whenever she thought about the ritual and what had occurred that magical night. She felt whole and complete since then. She felt unworried about the future and what was going to happen, it was like a deep peace had come over her. And it had been almost two weeks since the ritual! She also knew that when it was time, she would share with one of her sisters about what had happened.

Tonight was apparently that night.

As Allie was savoring the deliciousness of her pie, Alicia asked the question she had been avoiding asking all night, making sure to keep her eyes on her own delicious marionberry cobbler so as not to alert her sister.

"Sooooo…are we not talking about Justin anymore?"

This was Alicia's subtle way of talking about Justin again.

Allie laughed. "You are so hilarious. How long have you been waiting to ask me?"

"I wanted to give it some time after your headache meltdown. I didn't want to be responsible for launching you into another 3-day bout of repressed emotional mayhem. But you seem really good, in a happy-for-no-reason kind of way. Is that the BodyTalk or is there something else going on that you're not telling me about?"

Allie loved her sister so much. She always made her laugh and had the most irreverent way of addressing their life situations.

"Well, I appreciate you honoring the fact that I was in a sensitive state about Justin. But you are right, I do feel happy and maybe for no reason. It's sort of hard to explain and even I don't really have all of the answers. I know BodyTalk has helped – because I'm feeling my emotions instead of stuffing them down. And it's something else too..."

Allie's voice trailed off.

"What?" Alicia asked with a mouthful of Tillamook vanilla ice cream and cobbler. "Oh my god, you did it didn't you?"

Allie wished Alicia could realize how intuitive she really was.

"Did what?" Allie asked playfully.

"You know what. You did the ritual, didn't you? Of course Laney told me, and well, Brittany and Shelby too, that she told you to do it and she was hoping you would. Laney said that she had never done it before but had heard from others who had how powerful it was. Even Shelby's bestie Kathryn uses a similar ritual whenever there is disharmony in her relationship with Scott. Which I think is sort of creepy, but anyway. You did the ritual?! Tell me everything and for the love of god, how long have you been keeping this from us, and more importantly from me more specifically?"

While clearly nothing went on with one of the sisters without all of them knowing about it, Alicia and Allie did have a special bond that connected them in a deep, soulful way. It was a bond much like Laney and Shelby had. It allowed them to understand one another in ways that not everyone could and even when they couldn't understand, the love between them was so powerful that they would love one another through whatever it was. So of course Alicia assumed that Allie would share with her before she would the other sisters, giving her all of the juicy details. Besides Allie sort of owed it to Alicia after keeping her return back to the living from her divorce-coma a secret from everyone but Alicia. And even though Alicia was not necessarily "into" the spiritual path that Allie was now on and that Laney and Shelby were rooted in, she was like a voyeur who loved observing what her sisters were up to. Alicia had some sense that she would use the modalities and rituals when she felt it was the right time for her. For now, she was enjoying watching it all unfold before her with Allie and in the past with Laney and Shelby.

"I was keeping it to myself – it was so magical it was like I couldn't even give words to it. I haven't known how to explain it. But I did it about 2 weeks ago and it's like I can still feel the energy from it. "

"Okay, could you put that into Alicia-speak for me? I couldn't understand a single word that just came out of your mouth. Give me more details and more importantly – have you heard from Justin since you did it?

"I haven't. But I am totally okay with that. I feel this peace inside of me now. I know that everything is taken care of. I don't know how it will happen or what will occur, but I know that it is all working itself out. I haven't felt compelled to text, email or call him. It's like I can literally feel him with me Alicia." Allie leaned forward, pushing aside her cheesecake. Alicia raised her eyebrows, knowing that pushing aside Rosanna's chocolate chip cheesecake meant there was something really important happening. It was that good.

"Whoa girl. What do you mean you feel him with you?"

"It's like," Allie looked from one side to the next making sure no one was eavesdropping – she knew this topic was highly unusual and was bound to create some curious looks in her small town. "He is with me. Like I can feel his hand on mine when I sit down or when I'm driving I feel him in the seat next to me. When I'm cooking in the kitchen, I feel him alongside me chopping the onions. At night when I go to sleep, I feel him spooning me. He is there when I open my eyes in the morning, stroking my hair back and covering my face with kisses."

Alicia's eyes were wide with disbelief.

"Trust me, I know it sounds crazy, but it's true and it's totally happening. It's like my senses are incredibly heightened. It's like I don't need the physical him to do anything because the energetic him is already with me. I mean, it makes no sense at all but it also feels so right. He is already here and I am already there. The rest is up to the Universe."

Allie sat back in her chair and smiled. It was surreal speaking out loud what she had been experiencing the past couple of weeks. She knew they may sound like the words of a crazy woman, but she had never felt more connected and grounded. The ritual had done something incredibly powerful for her and just because her conscious mind couldn't fully understand it didn't make it any less real.

"Well, Allie, you're 100 percent right, it does sound straight up crazy. And if you weren't my sister and if Laney and Shelby weren't behind this woo-woo-ness I would consider taking you immediately to a doctor, preferably a highly trained psychiatrist. But it is you and I can see in your eyes that something big has changed." Alicia put her hands up. "So far be it from me to judge, if it feels good to you, then that's what matters. But yeah, you are officially in crazy town. Population — you."

Allie giggled. It *was* crazy town, but it was her crazy town. And she wouldn't trade what she was feeling for anything.

Alicia interrupted her thoughts. "So, are you going to tell Laney, Shelby and Brittany? Or do I get to?" Alicia was dying to get back at her sisters for being in on Allie's return when she hadn't been. That combined with a terrible habit of being unable to keep anything a secret meant Allie knew the time was severely limited between when the other girls would find out that she had indeed performed the ritual.

"I don't think we need to bother Shelby with anything right now, she is so close to giving birth. But I will tell Laney and Brittany at some point. Maybe text them? I don't know. It's like I still want more time with savoring the experience. I know Laney will want play by play details and I'm not sure I'm ready to give those up just yet. Think you could keep it to yourself awhile longer Lish?"

Alicia frowned. "Well you know it's not my specialty, but I will do my best. Maybe I can, I mean you can, tell them and then just say you don't want to talk about the details. And maybe your news will get Shelby into labor," she joked. "The last time I talked to her she said she felt like her and baby were ready to, and I quote, "get this show on the road." You know when Shelb starts using clichéd phrases that she has entered a very special time otherwise known as "I cannot take much more of this." If that kid doesn't hurry up and come out Shelb is liable to pull it right out herself."

Allie laughed. "She is so positive about everything it's hard for her to simply scream and say, "Get this kid out of me!" I love that her and Daniel are waiting to see whether it's a girl or a boy."

"Well from the medical world anyway. Let's not forget that they *have* consulted a shaman *and* an intuitive healer. They both feel they are having a girl, but the big reveal is sure to come soon. I wonder how fast we can get into Portland when we get the call?"

"Hmm…I was sort of thinking it might be more powerful for us to do a ritual at the ocean once we get the call that she has gone into labor. She is having a home birth, so she doesn't need all of us there. She needs to stay as calm and centered as possible. Mom will be there and so will Daniel, their midwife, her bestie Kathryn and Laney. I think any more people in the house would be too much. What if we did a special ceremony on the beach for the new human being they are bringing into the world?"

Alicia put her head in her hands. "Oh Allie. Are you going to be one of these people now? Performing rituals and ceremonies every time anything at all happens in the world? Good lord. Is this what it's coming to? Am I only going to be left with Bob for sarcasm and taking practical action? Because I don't think I can handle that Allie. I don't think it can be just me and Bob the stepdad who are quote-un-quote normal," Alicia added a nice dramatic flair by pushing away her cobbler in mock disgust.

Allie shook her head from side to side. "I'm afraid to report that yes Alicia, yes, I am now one of those people. But get on the train sister because you are pretty much outnumbered. Me, Laney and Shelby all get the power of this. Brittany isn't far behind, I'm certain of it. All the cool kids are doing it Alicia. Better get on board. Because you're right, you don't want to be drinking Bud Light with Bob while the rest of us live in Magic."

Alicia snorted and crossed her arms. "Crazy hippies." She sighed. "But you guys are having a lot more fun than the rest of us." She huffed again. "Fine. Crazy baby ritual wins. I'm in."

———

It wasn't long until Alicia's themed 'crazy baby ritual' needed to be put into effect. Allie was running on the beach late one afternoon when she got the call. She had been ramping up the volume on her phone after talking with Shelby and Daniel earlier in the week. They had mentioned that Shelby was having Braxton Hicks contractions and they knew their little girl would be entering the world sooner rather than later. Shelby had sounded calmer than she had before.

"There is just this incredible peace that has washed over me this week. Like I know she is getting ready to enter the world and it's time and everything is going to be okay. I don't know how to describe it, but it's this beautiful knowing I have," Shelby reported.

"Allie, she is seriously almost floating instead of waddling. It's like her whole energy field has changed now that we are only what appears to be days away from the birth of our little girl. I'm in so much awe of your sister," Daniel had gushed.

Allie loved how much Daniel loved Shelby. It inspired her because she knew that level of love was available to her and to everyone.

So when her phone's song of Drunk in Love by Beyoncé came on (she was going through a Beyoncé phase, and she wanted to keep the love theme all around her to support the ritual process) and she saw it was Daniel, she knew it was time. "Daniel?"

"It's go time. Shelby has been in labor throughout the day. Her team has been showing up and we've been taking things hour by hour and sometimes minute by minute which is why we didn't call everyone at once. She didn't want a rush of energy fueling the contractions. But now, Laney, your mom and Kathryn are here and so is our midwife. The midwife says she's getting close to being able to push. Shelby's doing really great, I'm so proud of her Allie. She gave me the go ahead to call you and have you let the other girls know what's going on. And we would love it if you would begin the ocean ritual you had mentioned to support our baby girl in coming into the world."

Allie felt her eyes well with tears. "I'm on it. And I am with you both in Spirit. I see Shelby's birth process flowing with ease and grace. I see her surrounded by all of her angels and guides of the highest light and I see your baby girl coming into the world blissfully." Allie wasn't sure who she was now, but ever since her experience with that ritual, she looked at the world in a whole new way.

"We'll call all of you girls once our baby has arrived. In the meantime, please let the other girls know to send peace, love and light. We are all set." Daniel's voice cracked and Allie could feel the well of emotions coursing through him.

"I love you both so much. Go support your loves Daniel."

"Thank you Allie. I feel so blessed to have your sister as the love of my life and to be bringing this child into the world with her – whether it turns out to be little girl or a little boy. Thank you," Daniel's voice broke as the tears came through.

"Daniel, we are so blessed that you love Shelby so much and are the father of this amazing new being. I'll take care of the girls and we'll talk and see you both once you're all on the other side of this and are proud parents."

She could hear Daniel sigh in gratitude and she visualized pink light surrounding him. Then, as soon as they hung up, she called Brittany and Alicia. "Girls, Shelby has been in labor most of the day and is getting close to being able to push her little one out. Daniel, her midwife, her bestie Kathryn, mom and Laney are all there. Surprisingly, as it turns out, our family *can* keep some things to themselves. Mom and Laney didn't say a word – Shelby didn't want too much energy directed at her as soon as she went into labor and everyone respected that wish. Laney will call us once baby girl is with us. Or at least if all of the intuitives are right – they will be having a girl. We never know – the Universe might surprise us, but until then we are going to act as if they are having a girl. Daniel is asking that we girls send love, light and peace to all of them. I'm at the beach and I'm going to begin the birth ritual. Alicia – can you light some candles in honor of the baby and do a brief meditation or prayer for her easy and divinely guided entry into the world? Brittany – can you do the same?"

Although Allie was half expecting Alicia to squawk, she didn't. Both girls were on board.

"We're going to have a niece! We're going to be aunties!" Brittany was crying and ecstatic at the same time.

For some reason the entering of this Soul into the world was causing all of the girls to well up with emotions of gratitude and love.

"Well, I don't cry or ritual for any baby coming into the world but there must be something really special about this one, because I can't stop the tears and I am totally game on for my part of the ritual," said Alicia.

"Okay girls, let's do this, let's support Shelby and her baby girl in coming into this world in the highest possible vibration. Laney will call us with more. In the meantime, let's do our part and we can check in with one another via text."

The plan was set and Allie felt a tingling sensation from the base of her spine up to the top point of her head. Something truly magical was at work. She ran back to her car to grab her lighter, incense, a blanket and sweatshirt – she had added all of that to her car since her conversation earlier in the week with Daniel & Shelby. The sun would be setting soon and she wanted to be prepared. It was incredibly synchronistic that

Shelby's baby's birth was starting at the same time the sun was setting over the ocean. *Divine synchronicity*, Allie heard. She wasn't sure from where, but ever since her ritual she felt more open to hearing and receiving whatever high vibrational message wanted to come through.

As she began to walk back out to the beach, she felt herself guided to walk through the small tunnel that led to a more remote beach for the ritual. It would also put her right in alignment with the sun setting. As she made the trek across the Oceanside beach and through the tunnel, it felt as though more Souls were gathering around and walking with her. Chills covered her body and tears trickled down her face, something really special was happening she knew that for sure. She also couldn't help but feel that Justin was with her as well. His energy had remained with her off and on throughout her days since the ritual and as she walked to the perfect spot on the beach, she felt him with her again.

When she felt like she had come to exactly the right place for the ritual, she laid out the blanket, put on her pink Love sweatshirt and sat crossed legged. She tapped Cortices, took several deep breaths and knew that somehow she would know exactly what to say and do, even though she had no real idea what she would be doing. She let her intuition guide her, as she lit the sage incense and began to wave it all around her, humming a tune she couldn't quite place. She rose and continued humming the tune and waved the incense stick as she walked along the water's edge.

I am now calling in the guides and angels of the highest light to be with me now. I am calling in the guides and angels of the highest light for Shelby, Daniel and baby girl – or boy – Allie corrected herself since technically the baby's sex was unknown – *to surround them where they are now.*

The wind picked up speed and blew her hair back and with such force she had to stop walking. She let the wind cover and caress her face, and she closed eyes and smiled. She knew they were all around her. All of her guides and angels were there, and they were using nature's tools to respond to her. She turned and faced the ocean, bringing her hands into prayer position in front of her heart, the incense wand continuing to burn.

I am calling in divine blessings for this new life that is about to grace the presence of all whom she or he meets. I am calling in divine blessings for Shelby and for Daniel. May Shelby's body relax with ease and allow this new life to flow out of her with bliss and grace. May all in the room feel the divinity that is present among them and may they honor the new life force energy that is before them with divine love. I am calling in the highest vibrational support possible for all involved in the bringing of this new child into the world.

Shelby began to walk, incense in hand back to her spot on the blanket as the sun sank further into the ocean. She heard a song begin to play, she couldn't quite grasp it, but it was soft and tender. She strained her ears and heard the faint but familiar tune of Blue Ocean Floor by Justin Timberlake. She didn't know what that could possibly have to do with Shelby's baby or the ritual she was performing. But she let herself hum the tune as she came back to her ritual spot.

Thank you oh great divine Ones in blessing Shelby, Daniel and their new baby. May their lives all be graced with abundance, success and love that allows them all to go higher than ever before while inspiring others to do the same. May they know the true divinity that they are and feel the bliss that they are meant to experience in this life.

All of this I ask with humbled honor of the great-ness of this life. Thank you a million times over. Thank you. I love you. Amen.

The wind picked up again as Allie raised the incense stick over the top of her head, to her heart and then to her root.

The ritual was complete.

Even so though, she could still hear the Blue Ocean Floor song, it seemed to pick up volume in her mind and all around her. She strained to connect the lyrics. What were they trying to tell her?

I hear it loud and you fall in the deep and I'll always find you
If my red eyes don't see you anymore
And I can't hear you through the white noise

Just send your heartbeat
I'll go to the blue ocean floor
Where they'll find us no more
On that blue ocean floor
On that blue ocean floor
On that blue ocean floor
On that blue ocean floor
On that blue ocean floor
Justin.

She could feel him again. Stronger this time. She closed her eyes. Perhaps his Soul was supporting the ritual and sending her a message at the same time. She took deep breaths and tried to connect with him energetically. She couldn't quite feel him but she knew something was shifting, she just didn't know what. Images began to flash in her mind of them together. In her kitchen, walking on her favorite beach, on this beach, on him holding a baby, of her cooking for him. They picked up in intensity as she heard Justin Timberlake sing:

20,000 leagues away, catch up to you on the same day
Travel at the speed of light, thinking the same thought at the same time

Heart beats at a steady pace, I'll let the rhythm show me the way
No one can find us here, fade out and disappear
Justin.

Hands touched her shoulders and she shuddered. Her eyes popped open. This wasn't Spirit, it wasn't fantasy, some man's hands were actually on her shoulders. Carefully she tipped her head back to see who was behind her.

Her face broke into a huge smile as her eyes met Justin's. She couldn't breathe. He was there with her. Right there, in the flesh.

Their eyes met and he said gently, "Hi."

He came around in front of her and embraced her, his strong arms taking her in and letting her body fully sink into his. Tears began to form and Allie felt herself give in to her emotions, holding on to him tightly, breathing him in. "You're here," she breathed out in between sobs.

"I'm here," he said as he stroked her hair and squeezed her into him.

They held one another like that for minutes. Their bodies pressed up against one another, she on her knees leaning into him and he on his knees holding her, their heads buried in one another's neck. Allie could feel her heart pounding so wildly and noticed that she couldn't tell the difference between his heartbeat and hers.

Finally, he pulled back, locking eyes with her, keeping his arms holding on to hers.

"I woke up and knew I had to come to you. I had to see you. I had been feeling you so strongly with me for weeks now. But I had closed myself off to you because my pain was too great. After you weren't able to say "I love you" – I shut down completely and began to indulge in my old fantasy that I needed to sell everything and move to India to live a life of service and solitude, and that relationship was not meant to be part of my life's journey. I totally compartmentalized what we shared and put all of my focus over the past 2 months into this fantasy that to truly give back I had to sacrifice everything for some greater cause. I got so close to going through with it too Allie."

Allie couldn't believe what Justin was sharing with her. That the pain of not hearing "I love you" from her caused him to shut down and almost leave her and the rest of the world for good. It broke her heart. Why would he think he could only be of service if he gave everything up? That sounded like poverty consciousness to her, but she wanted to give Justin plenty of space to finish what he needed to say. She was so relieved that he hadn't gone through with it and was instead in front of her, his hands holding hers tightly.

He continued. "In hindsight, I know it seems crazy. Extreme at best. Total martyrdom does not free one from feeling love. Giving of self totally is not truly giving, it's running away from what we are each here to do – to live the fullness of this human experience – and that includes loving and being in service. But my pain was so intense for me that I couldn't see this for some time. But then the Universe made sure I got the message. I was at the airport Allie, when I just happened to sit in front of a couple who was having a conversation about why we're here on this Earth. They were literally talking about what the purpose of life is. Like how is that even possible, right? It was the exact conversation that I needed to overhear."

"They were talking about how people run away from life – hiding out in their jobs, in extreme sports, in relationships that aren't truly intimate, in addiction – all in an effort to protect their hearts. Protect their hearts from being broken. And it just hit me. I was sitting there and my eyes welled up with tears and I knew I was no different. I had simply created a story that seemed more noble to me. That somehow if I gave everything up and only focused on service that somehow that would keep me safe and would be the "right" way to live. When in truth it was really about trying to escape pain. Escape true intimacy, escape from the possibility of discovering that I'm not truly lovable. And that is not living. Living is loving, and really showing up for another person. It's about living our truth and having fun and allowing life to be the best it can be. If I went to India under the guise that it would somehow make me noble to give up myself in that way, I would just be running away. I would have been running away from my destiny. I got up, turned to the couple and with tears in my eyes thanked them. They looked up at me blankly, but I swear to you Allie, those people were angels for me. I had gotten rid of most of my stuff, but had kept my place, with the intention of coming back every few months to see my family. I know now that that impulse was my intuition of my Soul trying to save me from walking away totally from the life I'm meant to be living."

Allie took a ragged deep breath. Here he was in front of her, pouring his heart out to her in a way she had never before experienced with him or with any man. He was admitting his erroneous conclusions about living a life of martyrdom. He was calling out the truth that running away, whether for a "noble" cause or not was still running away. And somehow, he hadn't. Somehow he had returned back to her. Allie couldn't help but admire his strength, his honesty and his innate hotness. She couldn't help but notice how he looked better than he ever had sitting there in front of her, the ocean behind him, the orange pink of the sky seeming to be on display only for them, only for their love.

Justin looked deep into her eyes and spoke again.

"I woke up the next morning not knowing what I would do or where I would go. I had kept part ownership in my businesses but didn't technically have to "be" anywhere. Your face," Justin raised his hand to lightly brush a few strands of Allie's hair back tenderly. "Your face had been popping into my consciousness despite my best efforts to completely shut you and what happened between us out. I had moments leading up to the time I went to the airport where I could just feel your presence with me. I would again brush it aside, but the morning after I turned back from India, something shifted and you were just *with* me. In that early morning moment, I knew I had to be with you. That I couldn't do anything but be with you. That every story I had told myself, every hurt I had manufactured — all of it was to keep myself safe. Because the thing I have been afraid of most is truly loving. Truly being loved. Experiencing the deepest, most profound intimacy available to me. And you, us, we could, we can be that. But I was too afraid and so I used my pain to keep us apart. I can't live like that anymore Allie. I just can't. I can't travel far enough away to keep myself insulated from true, deep loving. And finally I no longer think that is the answer. For the first time in my life I'm no longer looking to run away. In fact, I'm looking for the opposite."

Justin's eyes began to twinkle in the dusk. And Allie felt her heart begin to pick up speed.

"I need to dive in with you. I need to go deep with you. I need to see what is possible when I don't let my fear keep me from love. What happens when my love, when our love is opened up without bounds. I can keep myself closed off from you, from truly loving or I can dive in. I am diving in. I am diving in to you Allie, into us. Will you ever forgive me?"

Tears streamed down Allie's face as Justin spoke his truth to her. Her heart continued to beat wildly and her body coursed with love as she felt the depth of the truth he spoke to her. She smiled at the ridiculous yet so perfect way that they were both mirroring one another. That their fear had almost kept them apart forever. And now, now they could make a new choice. A choice to love one another. For all of eternity.

"Yes," was all Allie could get out in between tears. "Yessss."

Justin put his hand on the left side of her face and smiled back at her.

"Yes," he said. "Yes."

And with that he pressed his lips to hers, holding her face, holding her close, holding them together as one. Allie felt energetic fireworks shooting through her body as the intensity and power that Justin was bringing to her allowed her to relax into the pureness of their connection.

Justin pulled away, this time a small smile forming at his lips.

There was more.

"Allie, I knew from the moment I saw you at the yoga studio that you and I had a special connection. Our time together, albeit relatively short in terms of man-made time transformed me. Our disconnect helped to heal one of the biggest illusions I had held out for myself. Running away is no longer an option for me. I know that I love you. And I know that you are the woman I want to spend the rest of my life with. There is not a doubt in my mind. This time apart has taught me what is most valuable in my life and that when I allow myself to honor what I value most, anything is possible."

Justin lifted Allie up into a standing position, placing both of his hands on her face and kissing her softly. Allie couldn't stop the tears from running down her face and stopped trying. Her stomach began to dance as though butterflies were fluttering through it. Justin reached into his pocket and kneeled down on one knee.

Allie gasped, placing both of her hands over her mouth. She felt her body begin to shake and her heart and stomach begin to flutter in ways she had never felt her body move before. It was as though every cell in her body was singing the same song.

"Allie, will you marry me?"

Justin looked up at her, his eyes intent on hers, his question full of confidence and love and knowing. A knowing only a man who has a true connection to his heart and his path can have.

Allie's head began to bob up and down uncontrollably as she leaned down to kiss Justin.

"Yesssss," she spoke into his mouth. "Yesssss," she said over and over again, pulling him up with her into a standing position, and then pulling away, finally taking time to look at the gorgeous platinum ring with three tiers with 11 diamonds throughout, that he had placed on her finger.

Justin kissed the ring. "I bless this ring as I bless you and our life together," he said as he placed the ring on her finger. Allie beamed. She had never known a proposal or a man or a life could be as perfect as what she was experiencing. The ring was a perfect fit, of course. She admired it for roughly 3 seconds, and then she leaned in, grabbing Justin and kissing him more passionately than she had ever kissed any man before.

At that exact moment, her phone began to writhe in her pocket as Beyoncé's Drunk in Love played. They parted lips for a moment and she whispered, "A new Soul just entered the world."

11

Once the commitment to their connection was made by both Allie and Justin, it didn't take long for the rest of the details to work themselves out.

"I cannot believe I was feeling you with me during the same time frame that you were connecting to my Soul," Justin shook his head in mock disbelief as he helped Allie fold her clothes into her suitcase.

"Pretty magical, right? I can't believe you just woke up and were like, 'I'm going to Allie' and went and bought a diamond ring and hopped on a plane that same day. Now that's some empowered masculine energy. So sexy." Allie came over to where Justin was systematically packing her suitcase and wrapped her arms around his back, standing on her tip toes to kiss the back of his neck gently.

He stopped folding the clothes and leaned his head back. "Ah...now that I could get used to every day."

"I know, me too. That's why I love doing it. And...well, you just taste so good."

Justin turned to face Allie, wrapping his arms around her and pulling her close. His eyes looked down at her with desire. "You are too good Allie; you know that don't you?"

Allie leaned up on her tip-toes again to meet his lips. "I do know, yes." She let her hands run down the front of his strong chest and into his abdomen, letting her hands linger at the buttons of his pants. She couldn't help but notice her ring as she did this. In fact, she couldn't stop staring at it since Justin put it on her finger. Something about being his fiancé turned her on even more than his sexy neck, body and presence.

"We can finish packing later; you don't mind right?" she whispered as she breathed into his ear.

"All I care about is that you come back to Shorespoint with me and you don't need clothes for that," Justin said as he moved his hands up her sweater, unhooking her lavender strapless bra. As it fell off of her body, Justin's hands cupped her breasts softly.

Allie took a deep breath as she unbuttoned Justin's pants.

Seamlessly they moved together, disrobing each other, breathing in unison, becoming more and more vulnerable to one another on a deeper level. It was as if they had taken off one another's clothes for lifetimes as they moved together almost totally in sync.

Once they were both naked they pressed their bodies close to one another. Justin's hand moved to Allie's sacrum and another on her mid-back in her heart area. Allie placed her hands on Justin's sacrum and on the back of his neck. Her face lay on this chest and immediately their breathing synched up again as they breathed powerful life into each of their seven major chakras that ran up their spines.

It was something they had discussed doing during one of their Skype sessions before their break in communication and apparently, now was the time to put what they had discussed into practice. Allie focused in and saw both of their first chakras at the base of their spines lighting up a sparkling red hue, then an orange ball of light in their pelvis that seemed to be almost as large as Allie's bedroom – their sexual energy was so strong. Up into the yellow light in their abdomen or third chakra and then onto the beautiful expansive green light in their heart centers. They stopped for a moment there, both of them breathing heavily into their hearts, Allie's nipples were erect as the full power of her heart energy for Justin beamed into him and his into hers. After a few breaths they moved into their throat chakras and the blue light emanating from there was luminous, next was their third eye at the brow and the brilliant indigo light that allowed their intuition to be so strong. Strong enough for them to be thousands of miles apart but still feel one another. Their crown chakra breath almost seemed to blow them both away as the radiant white-violet light blasted into their crowns causing both of them to go weak in the knees. As the light softened, Allie could feel her and Justin's energy transform into an even more intense sexual energy.

She felt her yoni begin to pulsate with desire for Justin, just to feel him inside of her, to feel the completeness that their two bodies together created. Justin must have been feeling the same thing as he picked Allie up in one swoop and carried her to her couch which was free of the clothes and suitcases that had taken over her bed. Justin sat down carefully keeping Allie with him and she was overcome with awe at his strength as he lowered them both onto the couch.

She kissed him passionately letting him know how much his physical strength fueled her turn-on. As she did, she moved to straddle him, their bodies meeting in perfect alignment. Justin held her face and returned the intensity of her passion, creating an epic heat between them. A heat filled with passion, desire and unity.

Allie felt her yoni begging for him, wanting to devour him as quickly as possible. She tried to steady herself with her breath, but it was difficult if not impossible. Justin must have sensed this because he slowed down their kissing, whispering to her lightly "Breathe with me Allie, breathe." Allie anchored back to a deep breath filling her diaphragm on the inhale and letting her whole body soften on the exhale. Justin did the same, rooting in their sexual energy, softening it and slowing it down so they could enjoy each sensation more fully.

Justin leaned over to where his wallet was sitting on the end table, keeping his eyes on Allie the whole time. He slid out a condom and Allie burst into a smile. "You really do think of everything."

Justin smiled back. "Now you see that my choice of the couch was multi-faceted."

Allie loved how Justin took such good care of her. He was fully participating in their union; it wasn't something she had to do all by herself.

She carefully took the condom from him and began to unwrap it, keeping her eyes locked on him. She slowly placed it on the head of his lingam, rolling it down inch by inch. Justin breathed deeply as he watched her. Allie joined him with her breath to unite them before their physical merging.

She arched her body up to hover above him, placing both her hands on his face, kissing him tenderly, then easing back using her tongue to keep them connected. With their two tongues dancing around one another, Allie began to lower herself onto Justin. She did so slowly so she could feel every sensation of him penetrating her. Slower down and slower down still she went, their tongues connected as pleasurable sensations filled her entire body. She felt the desire to begin bucking him wildly, but held back, wanting to savor every bit of him slowly.

Justin's hands gripped her hips as he let her ground her yoni into him. He arched slightly up into her furthering the depth of their connection. As he did this, Allie pushed her chest into his, their nipples, and tongues connected at the same time as her yoni and his lingam. Electricity coursed up and down through Allie's body and she felt energy rushing into her crown. Justin's breathing was hard and labored as was Allie's – they were both trying to relax into the sensations in their bodies by opening to the depths of them more and more. With every orgasmic electrical impulse Allie imagined she was opening up her body to embrace it ever further, which caused it to course through her at an even more intense level. She moaned in pleasure as Justin arched into her more firmly, his hands gripping her hips lightly.

The energy was at an all-time fever pitch and they were barely moving. Allie was anchored down onto his lingam just feeling him, feeling every bit of him as fully as she could.

"Oh Allie," Justin moaned as she sat up more fully disconnecting their tongue and nipple connection. "I can't hold back much longer," he whispered into her ear.

"Me either," she whispered back, then locked eyes with him. She nodded her head and he nodded back, the desire in his eyes penetrating her almost as intensely as him inside of her.

Sitting face to face, Allie began to move, slowly grinding her clit into him, their eyes never leaving each other. She could feel the climax building inside of her; that the waves and waves of orgasm were ready to crescendo with Justin's orgasm.

Justin took over, lifting her hips up, bringing her up and down on him, slowly but firmly, all the way to the top of his lingam and then sliding all the way down until he was fully inside of her. It was then that Allie felt him, felt energetically the power of his climax coming for her. She nodded again and he breathed with her, extending his climax minutes longer for both of their pleasure.

Soon it was too much to hold back and both of them synched up their breath knowing that soon they would be creating a whole new world of energy with the intensity of their climax. Justin's hands gripped Allie's ass guiding her up and down his shaft, Allie's hands gripping his shoulders, never letting her eyes leave his as her body began to reach climax.

"Justin, Justin, Justin," Allie repeated his name again and again.

"Yes, yes, yes" was all he could say back to her.

The intensity built and soon they were both there. "Oohhh myyyyy goooodddddd," Justin cried as he arched into Allie and as Allie ground into him.

The waves of climax washed over both of their bodies from head to toe. As the waves began to recede, Allie continued to rock Justin's body, only at a slower rate like what she had begun with. She leaned in, connecting their nipples and tongues as another wave of orgasmic bliss shot through both of their bodies. Their breath re-synched and Allie laid her head in the crook of Justin's neck.

He placed one of his hands on her sacrum and on her heart. "Thank you Allie. Thank you."

Allie placed her hand on the back of his neck and slid her other hand on his sacrum. "Thank you."

———

"Don't worry I'm probably the only one who knows that the reason why you two are late is because you were having all kinds of wild sex," Alicia leaned in and whispered to Allie as she and Justin entered Daniel and Shelby's home in SE Portland.

Allie rolled her eyes and then smiled. It was true, her couch time with Justin had delayed them about an hour later than they had originally planned, but she knew her sisters would understand. She had text Shelby some excuse that there had been traffic on the drive to Portland. She should have known Alicia would sniff out the real story.

"Called it." Alicia said bouncing her hands up and down twirling through the hallway.

"Called what?" Laney said as she came around the corner to greet Allie and Justin.

"She's just being Alicia," Allie said smiling. She actually couldn't stop smiling; it didn't seem to matter what anyone said. Laney must have known what was going on as well as she burst into a huge smile and said, "We could say she's the crass one of the sisters but I think it's more accurate to say she's the intuitive one."

"Justin! Allie!" Shelby cheered as they walked into the living room.

Allie couldn't believe how much Shelby and Daniel were glowing. Shelby was cuddled up next to Daniel on the couch, their little girl Mia in her arms.

"Oh Shelby," Allie's hand moved to cover her mouth as tears filled her eyes. "She's gorgeous," Allie kneeled down to where they were sitting to get a closer look. Mia's tiny face was smooth and soft, a reddish blonde fuzz covering her small head and a delicate smile covering her face.

"She's like that most of the time, eyes closed and smiling," Daniel said. "It's simply the most beautiful thing I think I've ever seen, next to her mom that is." Daniel's eyes filled with tears. "I didn't know it was possible to love two women as much as I love Shelby and Mia."

Shelby leaned her head on Daniel's shoulder. "Really Allie, it's like the most incredible experience ever. I truly feel in every cell of my body that Daniel, Mia and I are a family. It's difficult to even describe – the feelings are so deep!"

"I cannot even imagine," Allie said as Mia gripped one of her fingers. "She is seriously perfect Shelby. I am so happy for you and Daniel, and Mia," she grinned. Allie leaned in to hug Shelby and as she did tears filled her eyes. She could feel the magnificence of this little being and she could see how Mia being in the world had further made Shelby and Daniel, and their connection more complete. It made her think back to when she connected with Justin's energy in the Soul ritual and the guidance she had heard about how their coming together made everything more whole. She could sense that it would be the same with bringing in a Soul that was destined to come into the world through pregnancy and then childbirth.

Allie looked up at Justin, his mouth open and tears in his eyes. She could see that he could also feel the power of this being entering all of their worlds.

Shelby must have noticed too as she said, "Justin, come here, I'm so sorry – everything is now solely about Mia, but it's so good to meet you." Justin grabbed Shelby's hand and leaned in and kissed her on the cheek. Allie stood up to stand beside him and as she did all of the sisters gathered around. It was then that Allie also noticed Shelby's best friend Kathryn and her husband Scott there as well.

"It's such an honor to meet you Shelby and be a witness to Mia's presence in the world. I'm frankly really overcome with emotion. I can feel the power of her being in the world and it feels really big." Justin stepped back and put his arm around Allie.

"It does feel really powerful that she is in the world – perfectly said Justin," Scott stepped in and shook his hand. "So happy you're here with us man."

"Me too, you have no idea how happy," Justin turned and smiled at Allie, kissing the top of her forehead.

Laney, Alicia and Brittany seemed to sigh in unison. "Forehead kiss, one of the best moves ever. This guy *is* good," Alicia mumbled.

Allie giggled and looked over at her sisters. She loved them so much. And she loved Justin so much and here they all were. Together.

Kathryn came over to them and introduced herself to Justin. "So Justin we're all dying to know what happened, what made you come here for Allie?"

Allie felt slightly protective of Justin but also knew that part of being in her family was being genuinely open and honest as well. With Shelby having the baby almost two weeks ago and being sequestered with Justin most of that time at the Coast, she hadn't been able to let everyone know what had happened.

"Geez Kathryn, get right to it," Brittany jokingly interjected.

"No really, what Kathryn said, we wanna hear. You two lovebirds have been locked up at Allie's and despite my attempt to peak into the windows to snoop I have no idea what is going on. So...spill it," Alicia said.

Daniel and Scott exchanged a knowing glance and looked over at Justin. "Sorry dude, this is how these ladies roll," Daniel said. "Why doesn't everyone sit down and get comfy and Justin let me get you and Allie a drink and then we can hear the whole story."

Justin laughed and shook his head. "I should have guessed this was coming with the way this one is," he joked as he nodded towards Allie. She smiled. He had no idea how right on he was.

"Welcome to the family, baby," she said as they cozied up on Shelby and Daniel's red plush carpet, placing pillows behind them so they could sit comfortably along with everyone else.

"I'm adopted family as Shelby's bestie, so I felt like I should break the ice," Kathryn smiled as Scott rubbed her shoulders in the large brown leather armchair they were now sitting in.

Daniel came back into the living room with a glass of Argyle Chardonnay for Allie and a Mirror Pond beer for Justin.

"So…here's what is really interesting…Justin came to me when I was on the beach doing the ritual blessing for Mia's birth."

All of the girls covered their mouths in awe. "Are you serious? No wonder he was so impacted by her energy," said Shelby.

Allie nodded, "I know! Mia has a very special connection to Justin and me somehow. Her birth happening at the same time he came to me, it feels like it's symbolic in some way of our relationship."

"A birthing of a new family," Laney said as she nodded her head.

"Whoa," Justin said "You ladies just took that to a whole other level that I had not even considered."

"Like we said, bro – welcome to the family," Scott said as he and Daniel nodded and laughed, reaching over to fist bump Justin.

"These women take everything to a level you never could have imagined," said Daniel. "It's like they were witches in a previous life or something."

The girls all went silent. Daniel had named something they hadn't even consciously considered but which felt eerily accurate.

"Now, you're the one taking things to a whole level we never imagined," Kathryn said as she looked around at the girls.

Shelby raised her arm up, the hairs on it standing on end, goosebumps covering it. "Anyone else having this reaction to Daniel's observation?"

Laney raised her arm, then Brittany, then Alicia. Allie could barely sit still goosebumps were covering her body so intensely.

"Holy shit," they all said in unison.

Silence filled the room as everyone's eyes went to Mia. "And Mia's the newest member," said Daniel. Shelby's eyes filled with tears. "Welcome to our witchy world lovely," she said as she leaned down and kissed Mia's head.

Everyone burst into laughter. "Well let's use our powers for good and have a rockin Welcome Mia, Allie's going-away and Engagement party then!" Alicia said as she raised her glass in a toast.

"Wait – Allie's moving?" Shelby asked perplexed.

"Wait – Allie's engaged?" Brittany jokingly asked. Allie had not wanted to steal Mia or Daniel and Shelby's exciting announcement with hers, so she had leaked out the engagement news to Laney, Alicia and Brittany first. And then just yesterday forwarded the text to Shelby, Daniel and her mom. She didn't want to make too big of a deal of it in the midst of Mia's birth, and she and Justin had decided to plan an engagement party at the Coast several months in the future.

Everyone laughed at Brittany's joke. Shelby cocked her head to one side and said lovingly, "Mia is happy to share the celebration with you two. I'm so bummed I got the delayed notice on the awesome news. So Allie – show us that ring!"

Alicia piped in, "Thank you! Allie told us we weren't allowed to make a big deal of it and so I've been side squinting at her finger since she walked in the door. Hand it over sis!"

Allie giggled and looked over at Justin who was beaming. "Show the girls honey – they want to see." Allie couldn't believe how much fun it was to be engaged to Justin and to be able to show her sisters not only her man but a symbol of their commitment to one another. The girls oohed and ahead over the ring and Allie even took it over to Mia so she could catch a glimpse, although her eyes were barely slits, Allie could have sworn she saw a small smile creep over her face.

"Uh, Allie, that's just gas – don't get too excited," Alicia teased. "Now let's move on to the next item on our agenda. You're moving? Getting engaged and leaving us? What's up with that?"

"Well first Alicia, before we go there, how about a big toast to YOU for being the one to tell Justin where I was at on the beach and then totally keeping it a secret from everyone? I am beyond impressed with you."

Alicia's face softened. "You all are starting to make me believe in true love. And keeping secrets. But don't get too used to it – I could let that new privacy/secrecy thang go at any time. I will not be held to a higher standard just yet. And…you're welcome Allie, I love you. But don't try to deflect from answering my question just yet." She turned her attention to Justin. "I help you out bro and now you're stealing her and she's moving? What up man?" Alicia mockingly gave her best bro impression.

Allie smiled and looked over at Justin. "Well, not forever," Justin sheepishly replied.

"Can we just toast and then get the whole story Alicia? There is actually a lot we need to know. Justin's story got one-upped by the engagement, so we need to go back to that too. Lots of ground to cover before we let you two out the door!" Brittany scolded.

"Okay, okay, fine, we'll toast, but I want the whole story," Shelby & Alicia said practically in unison, Alicia making sure to point directly at Justin and Allie.

"To Mia, the latest addition to our witchy coven and to Allie and Justin as they journey on together into the sunset with white light and a gorgeous gown," said Alicia. "To Mia & Allie," everyone cheered.

———

As the night wound down, and the group began to disburse, Allie and Justin reconnected out on Shelby & Daniel's patio to check in with one another.

"So, I know it's a lot, but this is my family. How are you doing with everyone and everything? Especially since they grilled you a little."

Justin laughed. "Really everyone was great and I can tell how much they love you. And Mia, wow, I am totally taken aback by how much I was affected by her energy. It's so powerful. And to know that she was coming into the world at the exact time I was coming back into yours and proposed. I mean, there are no words. It is truly magical."

"Well, babies are closer to Source energy than any of us so it makes sense that her energy is one of the most powerful you've experienced. But I've never felt anything like that before. I sense that she is going to have a special impact on all of our lives." Allie leaned in and wrapped her arms around Justin's neck, kissing it lightly.

He let his hands gently rub up and down her spine. "I totally agree. I feel really blessed to be part of your family Allie," he pulled his head back to look at her. "Thank you," he said.

Allie smiled and kissed him softly. "You are welcome. It is my honor."

"They did sort of grill me didn't they?"

"They really did," Allie laughed.

"First it was 'how could you not get back to her' – which granted, I had coming – and then on to what was I feeling and thinking as I came back to see you two weeks ago – nervous, but so excited of course and then on to how could I take you from them."

Allie interjected. "Which you were happy to point out had nothing to do with you taking me anywhere but rather that *we* were going to split our time between Oceanside and Shorespoint."

"Yes, that's right. I love how much they protect you. And really they could have been much worse. Don't think I'm not aware of that. I was sort of an ass."

Allie smiled up at him. "Yeah, sorta." Justin swatted her on the behind and then pulled her closer into him. "*But,*" she said with emphasis, "I am pretty sure they can see how happy I am with you, so that definitely helped your case."

"You think so?" Justin said as he leaned in to kiss her again.

"Okay you two cut it out!" Alicia announced as she walked into the room, fanning the air as though she was trying to clear out an evil energy. "I know you're madly in love and I know it's divine and I know that we are all celebrating your engagement and are super happy about it, but I don't have to see it every 10 seconds until you leave do I?"

Allie and Justin kept their arms around each other looking at Alicia's dramatic flair. "You better watch out girl, me, Kathryn, Shelby – you may be next."

Alicia scrunched her face. "I love men but I'm not so sure I want one for all of eternity. Because as you heard me say, I love men. Plural. Lots of 'em. Anyway, that's not why I'm back here, Mia is summoning you."

Allie and Justin looked back at each other and immediately booked it for Mia's room where Daniel and Shelby were.

"We just fed her and she is getting ready to sleep again but we would love to have you both do an in-person blessing for her before you leave," Shelby said, taking Allie and Justin's hands.

"Oh Shelby, what a beautiful idea. I would love to." She looked over at Justin. "What do you think?"

"I would love it if we could do a blessing as a couple over her. Would that be okay?" Justin responded.

Daniel put his hand on Justin's shoulder. "You fit into this family perfectly Justin. Absolutely, we would love that."

Allie and Shelby exchanged loving smiles. "I love that idea so much Justin, I think Mia will too," Allie said.

Daniel pointed to the candles set up around Mia's basinet. "We've saged the space and lit the candles, we'll leave you two to share your blessing with Mia."

Intuitively Allie went to the end of the basinet closest to Mia's head and Justin to her feet. "The masculine grounds, the feminine brings in the connection to Source," Allie murmured, nodding her head in delight.

Justin put both of his hands up over the lower half of Mia's body and Allie followed and did the same to the upper half. Justin spoke first.

"Dearest Mia, I bless you with a life of grace, ease and so much joy. I bless you with a strong connection to Source that lasts throughout your lifetime. I bless you with a powerful connection with your parents that allows all of you to work together to be in harmony with your individual and collective destinies. I bless you with a great love that surrounds you wherever you go. I bless you, the day you came into the world and your life to come."

Allie watched him carefully as she felt her heart fill with so much love for him that it seemed to have to stretch to make room for more and more love to flow through her.

Justin looked up at Allie and nodded to her.

"I bless you beautiful Mia with a deep desire to live your purpose and to bring your gifts to the world in a way that serves your highest good and the highest good of those around you. I bless you with the ability to use the power of your divine feminine energy to support you in all of your endeavors – to always allow life to flow to you with abundance and success. I bless you with a divine connection with your Beloved partner so that you two can create a love that is just as strong and powerful as your parents – knowing that this love radiates out into the world and changes the lives of everyone you meet. I bless you with the ability to follow your inner wisdom and guidance above all else for your entire life. And I bless you with the ability to feel the love that surrounds you right now in this moment and in every moment to come. I love you Mia."

Allie looked up at Justin and saw him beaming love to her. Their hands met, joined together over Mia's little body as energy surged through them both.

They looked at one another and nodded.

This was it. Their life together was beginning right alongside Mia's.

ESPECIALLY FOR YOU...

If you would like to stay in regular communication with Heather & the JOGs and receive a free training to support your Soul Living expansion, sign-up here: bitly/1C7y6CR

TELL OTHERS!

Did you love this book? Has it transformed your life? Tell the world about it with an Amazon review. Reviews make all of the difference especially with this level of leading edge work, and myself and the JOGs would so appreciate your kind words.

ADDITIONAL BOOKS BY HEATHER STRANG:

A Life Of Magic: An Oracle for Spirit-Led Living
http://amzn.to/1XL7jYu

A Life of Magic contains powerful, life-transforming transmissions from the JOGs — 5 non-physical guides that author Heather Strang was "introduced" to while at the John of God Casa in Brazil in 2013. The JOGs guided Heather to specifically create A Life of Magic as an Oracle so that more individuals can benefit from this Higher Consciousness perspective on living a truly magical and abundant Spirit-Led Life.

With this Oracle as your guide, you will no longer struggle or suffer to find the clarity you seek in your business, in your relationships, with money and in all areas of your life. Simply follow the practices outlined in this guide to be able to receive the answers to your questions in the Highest Light and with much ease.

After working with this Oracle, you'll receive:

- More clarity about what decisions to make in your life.
- Answers to your most pressing questions.

- Releasing of scarcity consciousness and stepping into greater Wealth consciousness.
- Increased vitality and energy.
- More Magic in your life – synchronicities, opportunities and the "right" people showing up as you are attuned to an increased level of Magic from the transmissions in this Oracle.
- Greater connection with your own Spirit Team and Source energy.

The Quest: A Tale of Desire & Magic
http://amzn.to/1Ngr4E4

Think True Love & Spirituality can't be hot?

For 30-year-old Kathryn Casey, merging the two has developed into a lifelong quest. A mind-blowing psychic prophecy sends Kathryn on a journey that melds meditation and wine, the Amazon and New Zealanders, hot sex and dark chocolate, and psychic healings complete with strappy sandals.

The Quest delves into the core of one woman's search for great love. This novel follows Kathryn throughout rainy Portland, OR, as she attempts to capture what she desires most, while avoiding the treacherous pitfalls of self-sabotage.

When Kathryn assumes she's found "The One" prophesized to enter her life, the Universe works tirelessly to bring her experiences and synchronicities that force her to think for herself. Along the way, she's visited by new and old friends alike who remind her that finding "The One" requires deeper insight into the self. Armed with this knowledge, Kathryn makes a shocking discovery that forces her to reconsider everything she thought to be true — from her lifelong quest to her desire to bypass motherhood.

Following Bliss
http://amzn.to/1QmIMWx

Get up at seven in the morning. Take shower. Go to work at Hello Portland. Pick up gluten-free cupcakes for Laney's party. Receive messages from the other side. Attempt to relay said messages to a sexy stranger. Get rejected.

This was not Shelby Hanson's typical to-do list. But it was exactly what was on the agenda for her one early fall day in Portland, Ore. Across town, Daniel Tillman was attempting his own impossible to-do list—to write a historical fiction novel with enough pizazz to win the heart of one of the nation's top literary agents, Kaley Hamilton, at the Willamette Writers Conference.

To an outsider, Shelby and Daniel's daily activities may appear ludicrous at best. In truth, they're both being led to love, romance and some wild nights in Maui.

Bet you didn't see that one coming...

Following Bliss gives readers a sneak peek into how who we love is often carefully orchestrated by the other side. Experience the fear, the excitement and the romance that causes Shelby and Daniel to collide into one another, and into the next chapter of their lives. Along the way, they lean on the support of Kathryn and Scott from The Quest: A Tale of Desire & Magic.

Following Bliss truly takes readers on a ride of romance and intrigue along with some sexy sightseeing. Mixing in chick-lit, visionary fiction and a side of paranormal romance—Following Bliss proves that there's so much more behind why we choose who we love.

Made in the USA
Middletown, DE
28 September 2022

11337679R00104